I0523089

JACE POWER

AND THE BATTLE OF MARS CITY

Jace was ecstatic. With the new sword and Da's note he suddenly felt confident. He walked to the spacious closet and stepped inside. *Well, Defender, what secrets do you possess*? Locating the hilt, he pressed the glowing emerald sensor. *Whoa*! Power rippled through the handle as a dazzling sapphire blade of light appeared, almost blinding him. *Awesome*! He turned it off immediately, placed it back on the shelf and stepped back into his room.

JACE POWER
AND THE BATTLE OF MARS CITY

RANDALL JAMES

This book is a work of fiction. All persons, places and events are either the product of the author's imagination or are used fictitiously. Resemblance to persons, living or dead, is entirely coincidental.

Text copyright © 2022 Randall James
All rights reserved.

Atlantic Breeze Books

No part of this book may be reproduced, or stored in a retrieval system, or transmitted in any form or by any means, electronic, mechanical, photocopying, recording, or otherwise, without express written permission of the author.

I would like to thank Silke for editing, graphic
artwork, and typesetting.

I would like to thank Dayna Plummer
for proofreading the final manuscript.

I would like to thank Mitzi Hathway
for reading the early chapters and for her
encouragement and support.

I would like to thank Nora Campbell for her
encouragement and support.

1

Career Day

2137

J ace Power felt like pulling a paper bag over his head. It was the last two weeks of school before Christmas break and usually a time for teachers and students to relax, but his eighth-grade homeroom teacher, Miss Townsend, had come up with the wonderful idea of Career Day. *Great.* That meant that a parent of each kid had to come to school and give a short speech about their job.

The problem was that Jace didn't think his parents had great jobs. His mother was a part-time cashier at Pharmamart, and his dad a sanitation engineer for NASA, which meant he piloted the old *Victory* spacecraft to the dark side of the moon once a week to deposit all of Eastern North America's garbage. These were not exactly stellar careers.

Of all the exciting new professions in the twenty-second century, being a refuse transport pilot was probably the least prestigious, and, well, Jace kind of held it against his dad. It was kind of embarrassing, except not 'kind of.' Other kids got to brag about what their mom or dad did, but not Jace.

Fifty years ago, Sydney's Greenport had been 'selected' as the collection site for all the waste from the East. Compacted garbage and recycling products arrived by ship, rail and drone. Spectacular Cape Breton Island (think green rolling hills filled with blueberries), which had once been the tourist capital of North America, was no longer on the cruise ship list of destinations. If the unsightly buildings didn't get you, the strong smells sure did. No matter what they used, scientists could never get rid of that ever-present stench. To Jace, it reeked of burning rubber and fish guts. *Ugh*! You could even smell it in New Waterford on some days, depending on the wind.

Because of the public stigma associated with Greenport, Jace's dad was sort-of-scorned by the small city of New Waterford, where Jace lived. For years the family made up a lie that his dad 'worked for the government,' but after a while, folks figured it out. In fact, some of Jace's *enemies* in town teased him by referring to his father as 'the garbage man.'

Miss Townsend, wearing a blue pantsuit and white blouse, rose and stood in front of the class. "Would someone like to share what their parent or guardian will speak about next week?"

A few kids raised their hands while Jace suddenly got an upset stomach and squirmed in his seat.

"Yes, Jenny?" Miss Townsend pointed to the prissy red-haired girl sitting towards the front.

"My dad, the owner of Caper Bots, is going to speak on robotics."

"Wonderful," said Miss Townsend, writing it on the digital blackboard behind her. She turned around again and surveyed the class. "Stephen?"

"My mom is going to talk about exploring the rings of Saturn. Her company is sending a drone in the spring to collect more data."

Of course.

"That will be very interesting," responded Miss Townsend, who filled in the time block on the blackboard.

She turned again and her eyes caught Jace's.

Uh, oh.

"How about you, Jace?"

He put on a brave face, but his voice was weak. "My dad is going to talk about waste management in space." Now this was a bit of a fib, as Jace had not actually told his parents about the school assignment just yet.

"What was that?" asked Mitch, a bulky dark-haired kid who sat two rows over. "I didn't quite hear what Jace said. Did he say that his dad was going to talk about being a *garbage man*?"

A few kids laughed and giggled as Jace turned red.

"That's enough, class," said Miss Townsend. "I think you heard him, Mitchell."

Helena, Jace's best friend, seated directly in front

of him, spun around, her brown hair flowing. "Don't listen to him, Jace." And even though he could always depend on Helena, and life would be unbearable at Breton Education Centre without her, Jace sunk deeper into his seat and wished again for a paper bag.

Jace lived with his mother in a two-bedroom titanium town-house, close to the ocean on Hudson Street. There were eight identical low-income buildings in this area of town, housing sixteen families. Five of the duplexes were on this side of the street and three on the other. The plain buildings had slightly different colours from each other — some beige and some light-blue, like Jace's.

This area of town was windswept, with a few trees dotted here and there. Jace's townhouse was right beside Central Elementary School — a red six-storey building, which had a parking lot and a large field for the children to play in.

New Waterford, founded upon coal mining and fishing about two hundred years ago, was now a small tech city of twenty thousand people. It was ten flight miles north-east of Sydney — population one hundred thousand — the major hub of Cape Breton.

It had snowed most of that day, and the streets of New Waterford were covered with about a foot of the white stuff. Christmas lights adorned most houses and gave the frigid winter nights some joy. The Powers had decorated their house, and multi-coloured lights hung around each window on the inside, while the holiday smell of spruce permeated the living room where the colourful tree sat in the corner.

That evening, Jace finally brought up Career Day during supper. The tasty meal just happened to be his favourite: fish sticks with smashed potatoes and ketchup. The bright kitchen, where cheery artwork hung on yellow walls, contained a round table covered with a blue tablecloth, along with an atomic stove and fridge.

His mom piled more fish onto his plate. "Are you going to ask your dad?"

"What about you, Ma? Can you come to school?"

His mom looked at the digital calendar on the fridge and shook her head. "Nope. I'm getting my hair done next Friday." She brushed a golden lock from over her eye and smiled. "Nick asked me out for supper and a movie."

"*Nick*? But I thought you weren't seeing him anymore." Jace disliked everything about Nick, a.k.a. *Mr. Slick*. Nick was handsome with sandy hair and brown eyes — and his teeth were way too shiny, even glistening. Jace was sure that Nick used one of those horrible teeth whiteners, which kind of made sense since he was a dentist. Jace felt that Nick was a phony, and Jace could just not understand why his mom couldn't see it.

He gazed at his mother for a moment. Jace resembled her with his light-brown hair, but whereas his mom had lively blue eyes, he had inherited his dad's emerald eyes and lanky frame. His parents had been separated for two years now and Jace still found it weird when she dated another man.

His mother ignored his comment. "You're seeing your dad this weekend, right? Ask him to give the talk. I'm sure he'd love to do it."

"Sure, Ma." Jace's V-watch rang and he hit the green button.

Helena appeared, her hazel eyes sparkling with excitement. "Hey, do you want to go snowboarding and look at lights?"

"Yeah, that'd be great. I'm just finishing up supper."

His mom smiled, giving him approval.

Five minutes later, Jace threw on his blue parka and black gloves, and dashed out the back portal with his board. "See you later, Ma."

Helena, who was slightly shorter than Jace, greeted him at the front of the driveway sporting a black coat with neon pink mittens and matching toque. It was pretty cold, but he didn't care. It was time for some fun! He clicked on the app, hopped on his atomic-powered board and took off, gliding on top of the snow-covered streets.

Jace's four-foot board was white with cool purple speed lines, while Helena's was white with fluorescent green markings. They cruised up and down each side street and then raced up Hudson which had a long open stretch. Hudson sloped up to Plummer Avenue, the main street of New Waterford, which was about half way to BEC. As they stopped and talked about the cool lights and decorations on a few of the houses, Jace could see Helena's breath.

Later, as they cruised back down Hudson, Jace gave a signal to go to the big empty field by the shore, just past the townhouses. As they came to a stop, Helena's board clipped the front of his and they tumbled into the snow. Jace ended up on top of her for a brief moment and they gazed into each other's eyes. She giggled. *Man, she's pretty,* he thought. Jace jumped up and offered his hand. She took it and hopped to her feet.

"Want to watch a movie this weekend?" Helena asked.

"I'd love to, but I'm spending the weekend with Da."

"Ah, too bad. Are you going to invite him for Career Day?"

Jace frowned. "I'm thinking about it, but Mitch is such a jerk."

She tapped his arm. "Don't let him get to you. He's just a bully. Your dad's a great guy."

"Yeah, he's pretty fun, actually." Jace looked at her. "Thanks, Helena. You really are a great friend."

She smiled and jumped on her board. "Race you home!"

As they sailed home, Jace thought about Helena and their growing relationship. She had always been a tomboy, playing hockey and all the sports with Jace and the neighbourhood kids through the years, but they were teens now and that was all changing. He wondered if she was having the same thoughts about him.

2

Weekend With Da

On Friday after school, Da pulled up to BEC in his sapphire Jag-Z and Jace hopped in.

"Hey, Sport, what's up?"

"Hey, Da. Why do you still have your lab coat on?"

"I do?" He looked down at himself in surprise and they both chuckled.

"It was pretty busy today at work and I was late getting off."

Jace smiled. With his messy black hair, white coat and pen protector, his dad reminded him of a mad scientist — a good one, of course. Ma had told him a few times that Da was *quirky*, and, so, Jace wondered often if he, too, was quirky. *What did that even really mean?* Jace just thought that his dad was funny and shy.

His dad drove through town and headed out the New Waterford highway towards Sydney. He lived in an old bungalow in Sydney River, a few minutes' drive from

Greenport.

"So what did you learn at school this week?" his father asked.

"Well, we actually have an assignment coming up next week, and one of our parents is supposed to come and talk about their career to the class for five minutes."

His dad broke into a nervous smile. "Do you want me to attend and speak or is your mom going to do it?"

Jace tried to hide his thoughts, as he knew it would hurt his dad. He might not have the best job in the world but he sure was one of the best dads, always taking the time to play sports with Jace through the years and being a pretty humble guy. If only he had another job — *any* other job — Jace thought that life wouldn't be too bad at the moment.

Jace glanced out his window. "I don't know yet."

"No worries, mate," kidded his dad. "By the way, I have to pop into work to check on something." His dad selected *flight* and they flew over the inlet to Greenport. From three hundred feet up, Jace viewed the sprawling site that contained about twenty grey and olive-coloured buildings from at least ten companies. Various climate and environmental agencies worked there besides the waste management that his father did, and a few of them burned different materials, which contributed to the awful stench. In fact, two smokestacks currently blew out pink and black vapours. Climate action groups often held protests just outside the facility.

After landing, his dad ran into the grey four-storey office building with the glowing *Greenport* graphic above the portal, and Jace selected his window down, hoping to get a little fresh air. After a couple of minutes, though, he could smell the waste and quickly put his window back up. *Ugh.* It didn't help that there was a huge fish processing plant right beside the facility where screaming seagulls often dug through the garbage. Five minutes later, his dad, wearing a black flight jacket, emerged and hopped into the car.

"I had to check on a few documents and instruments. I have a special delivery of nuclear materials and waste that I have to transport to the moon, *and soon.* No one wants it sitting around here."

"Special delivery?"

He nodded. "Yeah, I have a heavy load of plutonium and uranium. They're building a new reactor on our base. I have to fly on Tuesday and be out of the way for the big NASA mission on Wednesday."

"Oh, I forgot about that," said Jace. "That's going to be awesome!"

"Yup — NASA is going to obliterate the Titan asteroid with two Arrow missiles. It's going to be a great show — fireworks from space!"

"What happens if they miss, Da?"

"Miss?" His dad made a scary face. "Oh, nothing — just that Earth will be *destroyed*!"

Jace laughed. "Really?"

His dad rubbed his chin. "No. Well actually, yes — at least for those in the Great Lakes area. It could hit anywhere from Southern Ontario to Wisconsin." His dad smiled. "But they aren't going to miss, Jace. It's routine. Do you know the amount of tech that is on the Comet spacecraft and missiles, in addition to all the military satellites and telescopes? There's no way they're going to miss. Don't worry."

His father pointed towards the golden *Victory* that was sitting on the tarmac, partly covered in snow. "What a beauty, eh? They just gave it a fresh coat of metallic gold. It was starting to wear out, which is not good for radiation."

"Sure, Da." Jace tried not to roll his eyes. *The twenty-first century called and wants their spaceship back.* The *Victory*, purchased by Cape Breton from the British to win the NASA waste management contract, was an old cylindrical transport ship about one hundred feet long, with four storage bays. It had two wings, two tail fins that angled out and a cockpit for two astronauts, although for routine moon flights, one pilot could handle it.

Although atomic powered, the *Victory* was relatively slow compared to the sleek and modern Comets and other cool space ships. As he stared at the shiny old beast, Jace noticed workers and robots, with cranes and vehicles, loading it up with large titanium containers that had yellow-and-red nuclear warning signs on them. Father and son took off and arrived minutes later at his dad's blue house that sat on a small parcel of land. As they landed, Jace noticed the outdoor Christmas decorations.

His dad tapped his watch. "Christmas lights on." The multi-coloured lights along the roof edge and around the main window and portal came to life. Blinking lights also appeared on the giant snowman, penguin and candy cane sitting in the front yard.

Jace smiled. "*Cool.* You got everything up."

"Yup."

After enjoying the lights for a bit, they went inside, and Jace plopped down at the kitchen table.

"Hey, Sport, do you want to order us two pizzas?" asked his dad, removing his coat.

"Yeah! Thanks, Da!" Jace was famished and phoned Buddy's Pizza, ordering two large Hawaiians. Five minutes later, the front portal buzzed. Jace pressed the sensor and there stood a four-foot-tall Buddy bot. He had a white smooth round head, a chubby body (emblazoned with a blue Buddy's logo) and arms, as well as two stout legs for flying and landing. His face had the interactive graphics of a male teen with blue eyes. All the delivery bots were nick-named Buddy. Two packaged pizzas emerged from Buddy's stomach, which was actually an oven. Jace grabbed them, placed them on the living room coffee table and returned to the portal.

Da sauntered over to Buddy, while glancing at his watch. "So, what took so long?"

Jace grinned.

Buddy's eyes popped. "Oh, I'm *extremely* sorry, Mr. Power. I will speak with the cook and ensure—

"I'm just kidding, Buddy."

The bot pointed with his right hand. "Oh, Mr. Power, you are such a kidder. You get me every time. How would you like to pay?"

"Put it on my tab."

"Yes, sir." Whirring sounds emanated from Buddy's head as he calculated, followed by an awkward silence.

Da crossed his arms. "Is there anything else?"

Jace chuckled.

The bot looked up at Da. "No, sir. I just—

Da slapped his own forehead. "I almost forgot. Give yourself a five gocoin tip."

"*Five gocoins*?!" Mr. Power, that is *extremely generous* of you. I don't know what to say." More whirring sounds.

"You're welcome, Buddy. Enjoy, and we'll see you again in two weeks."

"Yes, sir. Thank you, sir."

Buddy turned around to fly off as Jace closed the portal and Da grabbed the soft drinks.

"That never gets old, Da." They chuckled and fist-bumped. That night they binge-watched old comedies in the living room after stuffing themselves with pizza and Neapolitan ice cream.

On Saturday morning, Jace woke up to the wonderful aroma of waffles and coffee and shuffled to the kitchen in his blue pajamas. His dad was standing by the toaster making waffles while a bunch stood on a big plate in the centre of the wooden table, set for two.

"Dig in, Sport, you're going to need your energy today."

Jace rubbed his eyes. "What? Why?"

"The pond is frozen over and I thought we could take some shots."

"Awesome! That'd be great." Jace kept a pair of skates and a hockey stick at his dad's.

"I've invited a friend to come along. I hope that's okay."

Jace poured some syrup on his waffles. "A friend?"

His dad joined him at the table. "Yeah, he's already here, sitting in the living room waiting for us."

"Huh?" Jace was still half asleep.

His father had a huge grin on his face.

Jace wolfed down another bite and walked into the living room.

"Da! You got *Maurice*!" Jace ran over and sat beside Maurice, who was sitting on the brown leather couch.

Laughing, his dad entered the living room.

Maurice was the hottest new gadget for Christmas! He was a four-foot tall robotic goaltender in full gear, cage mask and Montreal Canadiens sweater. You could buy the goaltender in any team jersey and he came with different names. Of course, Jace and his dad were big Leafs fans.

Maurice came with a smart net and puck, which stood by the Christmas tree in the corner. The net was red-rimmed with white netting. You could shoot pucks at the net and Maurice could do all the moves of a goalie, like a great glove save or kicking out a leg to make a pad save. Jace squeezed parts of Maurice, who was made of a soft-leather material. His insides contained moveable robotic parts.

"How does it work, Da?"

"You just have to set him up in front of the net, turn on the app and start firing pucks! He interacts based on the movement of the puck and where he is in relation to the net. Just think about it — our very own goaltender!"

Jace was ecstatic!

His dad stared at him. "Merry Christmas, Sport! I thought you could have this present early."

Jace rushed over and gave his dad a big hug and kiss. "Thanks, Da! This is one of the best gifts ever!"

"Super! Let's finish breakfast and head down to Cameron's pond. We might have to clear it off as there's been a lot of snow overnight." Father and son returned to the kitchen table and finished their breakfast. Jace couldn't wait to take shots at Maurice!

An hour later, sporting their Leafs jerseys over a couple of heavy sweaters, they sat on a big log on the edge of the pond and laced up their skates. Jace's jersey was white with blue trim, while his dad had a blue one with white trim. His dad grabbed the scraper (a board attached to a long stick) and skated around, clearing off a good chunk of the pond. Thankfully, no one else had arrived on this frigid blue-sky morning, so they had the ice all to themselves.

His dad set up the goal and Maurice while Jace skated over and brought their hockey sticks. When his dad turned the app on, the goalie's bright green eyes came to life and he got into a standard goalie position. They howled in glee!

"Here we go," said his dad, turning on the puck and dropping it. They skated around for a few minutes, just passing the puck back and forth, and then Jace broke in on the goalie and rifled a shot towards the top right corner. Maurice raised his glove to stop it, but was too slow as the puck hit the back of the net.

"He shoots. He scores!" hollered his dad. Jace passed the puck back to his father who came in on Maurice, faked a shot, went to his left and backhanded it into the open net.

"This is so cool!" shrieked Jace.

"I know! He's a bit slow, but it's working great." The next hour was hockey paradise for father, son, and their new buddy, Maurice. Afterwards, they trudged back home through the snow and his dad made them hot chocolate. Jace's fingers were frozen, but he didn't care. It had been such a blast!

Later that night, Da made spaghetti and meatballs and they watched some old Leafs highlights from the twentieth century. They loved watching those old hockey games. That's where Jace had learned about the disgruntled fans wearing paper bags over their heads. It was hilarious.

The rest of the weekend went by like a flash, as usual, and on Sunday evening Jace was back home. Father and son sat in the Jag in the driveway.

"Have a great week, Jace, and I'll see you on Friday for the class talk. Don't worry. I'll try not to embarrass you."

Jace felt bad. "I won't be embarrassed, Da."

His dad ruffled his hair. "You know I love you, Sport. And I always miss you like crazy after I drop you off and drive back home."

"Ah, Da. I love and miss you too. Always." They both leaned over and hugged.

As Jace hopped out and headed for the back portal, he looked in the main window and saw his mom waving to his dad. He snapped his head back to see his dad waving also — both of them smiling. He had a quick thought about how great it would be if his parents were still together, but his mother had gone over it with him a few times — and told Jace it was impossible. They had just grown apart. Jace waved again to his dad as the car motored up Hudson Street.

3

Florida, We Have a Problem

Big flakes continued to fall on Tuesday morning as Jace and Helena rode their snowboards to school. Some of the snowdrifts were a few feet high and even higher on the sidewalks because of the droneplows.

"I wonder if they're going to cancel school soon?" asked Helena.

"Yeah, I wonder."

Just then, Jace's watch rang and his dad appeared, so they stopped on the sidewalk.

Jace moved his arm to catch Helena on his watch. "Hey, Da, look who's here."

"Hey, Helena!"

"Hey, Luke!"

"Just a quick call, Sport. Everything is loaded up on *Victory*. I'm taking off in a few minutes and should be back late Thursday. Love ya."

"Sounds great, Da. Love you too."

They both made the *love you* sign with their hands

and his dad ended the call.

Jace looked at Helena. "He's taking some nuclear materials on this trip."

"Cool."

At that instant, someone smashed into Jace from behind, launching him face-first into a high snow bank.

"Hey!" Jace wiped snow off his face as he turned around. It was Mitch and his goons!

Mitch grinned. "Sorry about that, buddy. You should watch where you're going."

Jace stood up with Helena's help. "Take a hike, *creep*."

Mitch jumped off his board and grabbed Jace by the scruff of the neck. "Who you calling creep, *creep*?" Mitch's two buddies laughed. Mitch was kind of big and Jace wasn't much of a fighter, so he just stood there, hoping Mitch would move on.

Suddenly, Helena got in Mitch's face. "You heard him. Leave him alone, *creep*!"

"Butt out."

"Nope, sorry. I don't butt out with bullies!"

By this point, tons of kids on their way to school gathered around the unfolding drama. Mitch, who suddenly looked unsure of himself, let go of Jace and glared at Helena. "I don't fight with girls."

"Why not?" Helena wasn't backing down an inch.

"Well, 'cause ... 'cause."

"Yeah?"

"Because you're a girl."

Helena laughed. "You're not too bright are you Mitch?"

Some of the kids started to laugh at Mitch.

"Hey — stop it."

Helena crossed her arms. "Oh, you don't like being teased? How interesting. You know what they say about bullies, Mitch?"

Mitch's eyes darted from Helena to the other kids.

She pointed to her head. "They say bullies aren't *really intelligent* so they have to pick on others to show everyone how tough they are. Is that true, Mitch?"

Most of the kids burst out laughing.

"Whatever. Let's go, guys." Mitch and his gang took off to the sound of cheers and jeers!

Some of the kids patted Jace and Helena on the back as they passed by.

Jace brushed himself off. "Thanks."

Helena smiled. "No worries. I was hoping he'd take me on so I could show him my latest Jiu-Jitsu moves."

Jace chuckled. "I'd love to see that. Based on our matches, I'd put my money on you."

They fist-bumped.

The rest of the day passed without incident as the snow continued to fall.

On Wednesday morning, the whole school gathered in the main auditorium on the second floor to watch the NASA mission to destroy Titan and save Earth.

Being so close to Christmas break, it was a festive atmosphere. A giant screen hung from the ceiling above the stage where the principal and teachers had gathered.

The high school was a seven-storey building made out of titanium and brick with lots of windows for each class. One of the fun things about BEC was the transparent elevators. A main circular one rose up through the centre of the building, while smaller ones hung on the outside of the school on each side, giving great views of the town and ocean.

Helena sat beside Jace towards the back of the room. "This is going to be great."

"Yeah!" They fist-bumped.

The chubby principal, Mr. Odo, gave a short talk and then turned up the volume on the NASA channel. The NASA director in Cape Canaveral, Florida, a stocky bald man in a white shirt and dark tie, explained the mission and showed some pretty cool graphics about how the sleek silver-and-blue Comet spacecraft would fire its two missiles into the giant rock and blow it to smithereens.

The metallic asteroid, named Titan for its massive size, was about five thousand feet wide. Some smaller fragments would hit the moon and a few would reach the Earth, but would result in only a wonderful light show. The astronauts would, of course, be international heroes, and Jace wished that his dad was one of them.

An amazing backdrop to the Cape Canaveral video

was that it was snowing in Florida. It was actually snowing down the entire east coast, from Nova Scotia to The Sunshine State. The white stuff clung to the spacecraft and most of the NASA equipment. *Cool.*

The two astronauts, a man and a woman in blue suits and helmets with black face-shields, waved to the audience and entered the spaceship. A red-and-white Arrow missile hung off each wing-tip. A few minutes later, the school joined the countdown along with the rest of Canada, America and the world. The whole planet was watching. Soon, the dual rocket engines ignited and the spacecraft raced down the tarmac and lifted off. A few thousand feet up, the atomic engines kicked in and it streaked upwards. The spacecraft rose higher and higher and became smaller and smaller. Suddenly, there was a loud *BANG* and the giant screen went black.

A collective gasp filled the room, followed by tons of chatter.

Helena grabbed Jace's arm. "What was that?"

Jace shook his head. "I have no idea."

The teachers and the principal huddled together at the front for a few minutes, when abruptly the screen reset and everyone stared at the shaken NASA director. "Dear friends, I regret to inform you that the Comet spaceship has exploded just before leaving the atmosphere. Thankfully, the onboard computer ejected the astronauts before the blast. It appears that one of the missiles ignited accidentally. We're examining our back-up options as we speak and will release a statement within the next hour. Out."

The screen went black again and the principal told the students to return to their home-room classes. Miss Townsend just let the class talk and eat treats for the next half hour. After receiving a call, she announced that everyone was to head back to the auditorium for an important announcement. The students and staff returned to where they were before and the screen was powered up again.

Surprisingly, President Franklin of the United States appeared onscreen. The popular leader, about fifty years of age, had mid-length brown hair and sported a magenta pantsuit. She normally was bright and cheerful, but today looked sombre. "Dear Friends, the severe weather conditions, the worst for fifty years, has knocked out our backup plans. Some of our equipment and computers are shut down because of the frigid temperatures and we cannot get another Comet ready in time for this mission. In addition, the ISS has informed us that Titan is travelling much faster than expected. We asked, but the UK, Japan and Europe have nothing ready at this moment. Our managers have told us that we have only one option remaining, which the NASA director will explain to you momentarily.

"In the next few hours we are going to evacuate cities closest to the Great Lakes in Wisconsin, Illinois,

Northern Michigan and Southern Ontario. We'll be sending out alerts immediately. Drones will be scheduled to take those who don't have access to flight vehicles to safety. I ask each of you watching to pray for our planet, especially the affected areas."

The screen switched to the NASA director: "We have spoken to our colleagues in Canada, and Captain Power from the" — he checked his notes — "Cape Breton Greenport — Captain Power is currently on the dark side of the moon depositing nuclear materials with the *Victory* transport spacecraft, and our scientists and engineers have determined that we should be able to crash the *Victory*, loaded with plutonium and other elements, into Titan. It should act as a gigantic nuclear bomb — shattering the asteroid, and knocking it off course. Based on our calculations, it is the only chance we have, and time is of the essence."

Captain Power from Greenport. Jace couldn't believe his ears. They were talking about *Da*! Everyone in the auditorium turned towards Jace. It was like a slow-motion scene. His head was spinning. Helena leaned into him for support.

Almost immediately his watch rang. It was his mom. "I saw it, Jace. I'm coming to pick you up right away. Meet me outside."

"Yes, Ma."

Jace looked at Helena. "This is crazy."

"I know."

As the whole school buzzed, Jace and Helena

walked out into the hallway towards the main elevator.

They stopped and gazed into each other's eyes.

"I have to go," Jace said, as he waved his hand over the sensor.

Helena suddenly kissed him. It was a peck on the cheek but brushed his lips. Jace walked out the front portal of BEC, touching his lips and trying to understand everything that was happening. All he knew was, his dad was in grave danger and Helena had just kissed him. *Crazy.*

Five minutes later, he was sitting in the car with his mom.

"The Prime Minister just called me," she said.

"The *Prime Minister*?"

"Yes. Canada and the US are working closely on this. He said that there is no time for your dad to call you. Plus, as you know, communications are very poor on the dark side of the moon. He has to load up and rocket towards the asteroid immediately. Your dad and his colleagues were in the middle of unloading all the material when they got the call."

"But, but ...." Jace's eyes welled up.

His mom hugged him tight. "I know, Jace. We're going to have to trust."

Jace looked at her. "When is it going to happen?"

"I don't know. Later today, I think. Someone will call us. I think that NASA might show it. Not sure, because ...."

Jace knew what that meant. NASA might not want

to show someone getting obliterated while saving the planet. But that *someone* was his dad. Jace suddenly thought about all the times he had been embarrassed about his dad's job and felt stupid.

Later in the afternoon, someone from NASA called Ma and went over all that was about to transpire. The event was going to happen that night around seven Atlantic Time. It was surreal. The whole world was going to watch his dad smash the *Victory* into Titan and save North America — if it actually worked.

4

Da vs. Titan

Jace's emotions were all over the place. His dad was going to die, which Jace really couldn't fathom, and, yet, he was also going to be an international hero and save North America. His mom invited Helena over to watch the event. She sat beside Jace on the black sofa in the living room as he scrolled through photos and videos of his dad on his watch and shared them with her. Just before seven, his mother entered the living room and flicked on the large screen in the wall and sat down on the other side of Jace, who couldn't believe he was viewing this in real time.

"There's the *Victory*," announced his mom. The golden spacecraft, which looked tiny on the screen from this view, raced towards the giant red-and-grey metallic asteroid that was barrelling towards the Earth — about 400,000 miles away. Titan, which was shaped somewhat like a rectangle with jagged sides, was going to just miss the moon by a few thousand miles.

The silence was deafening as there was no commentary at this point. Jace couldn't see his father, but imagined him with a look of determination on his face. As the *Victory* closed in on Titan, Jace said a quick prayer for his dad. He didn't really know what to say, but just asked God to help him. When he opened his eyes he caught a glimpse of the impact and the tremendous explosion, with hundreds of chunks of the asteroid flying off in different directions, some screaming towards the ISS camera.

Love you, Da. His dad had done it. The *Victory* was no more. Tears streamed down Jace's face as his mother wrapped her arms around him and Helena held his hand. Not only was Jace overcome with a sense of loss, but he felt bad, again, that he had secretly held his father in such low esteem over his job. Of course he knew that his dad was not actually his job, but he had let bullies convince him otherwise. Amazingly, it was that very work that had propelled his dad to complete one of the greatest feats in Earth's history. That thought brought a smile to Jace's lips even as he tasted tears.

"I'm so sorry, Jace." His mom hugged him tight.

A female voice on NASA News announced that Titan's trajectory had changed. He could hear his neighbourhood yell with joy. They would know within the hour if any parts of the asteroid would still impact Earth or pass harmlessly by.

Da vs. Titan

Over the next couple of hours, lots of neighbours dropped by to comfort Jace and his mom. Helena's mother, Barb, who resembled Helena and was close friends with his mom, came over and had a cup of tea with her in the kitchen. Helena snuggled up to Jace and didn't say a word as he continued to scroll through photos and videos of his dad. At one point, Prime Minister Ferguson called his mom and she stood in the entrance to the living room and relayed his congratulations and condolences to Jace. The rest of the evening was just a blur and he went to bed early after everyone had left.

Waking up in the middle of the night, Jace rose, went to the window, and gazed upon the starry sky. Looking out over the ocean, he saw a couple of shooting stars and realized that they were the last remnants of Titan. He smiled as his forehead rested on the cold window-pane. "Love you, Da," he whispered.

The next morning, as more friends and relatives dropped by to chat and offer condolences, Jace printed out his favourite photos of his father and placed them on the coffee table in the living room, finding frames for some of them. His mom had said they should celebrate his dad's life instead of feeling bad about his passing. Just before lunch, Barb arrived and helped his mom prepare sandwiches and desserts for the guests.

A bit later, his mother, wearing a grey sweater and blue pants, entered the living room and checked out the display of photos that he'd made. A few of the photos were of all three of them from a few years ago — one from a ski weekend at Ben Eoin, which she picked up. She sat down beside Jace and they gazed at the photo, which she lightly brushed as she spoke about it. "That was such a great time."

"Yeah. Remember when Da wiped out on the first trip down the hill?"

She laughed. "Who could forget?"

At that moment, her watch rang. Jace looked over and saw that it was Nick. His mom tapped the red button instead of the green, which sent Nick to the messages.

Yes!

They looked at the photo a while longer and then she placed it back on the table and headed to the kitchen. The visitors helped Jace to deal with his loss, as a few of the adults told him stories about his father; things he never knew — like what a stellar pilot he had been in the Canadian Air Force before he got out and became a civilian. Every story seemed to talk about how humble and nice he was.

At about one o'clock, as Jace sat in the living room, his mom entered with a handsome Black man of around thirty-five years of age, wearing a navy-blue suit and light-blue tie.

"Jace, this is Pastor Lawrence."

"Hi."

"Hey, Jace. Nice to meet you. I've heard a lot about you from your dad."

"My dad?"

His mom went to the kitchen.

"Yes, your dad attended our church: Grace Baptist in Sydney. He didn't come every week, but about once a month. He liked the Sunday night services, where we have a worship band. We've had some great chats over coffee and he talked about you often. I wanted you to know that."

Jace put his head down as his eyes welled up again. Pastor Lawrence sat down beside him and put a hand on his shoulder.

Jace glanced at the pastor through his bangs. "Is Da in Heaven right now?"

The pastor put his hands together and thought for a moment. "Well, the Bible says that whoever believes in Jesus has everlasting life. Luke certainly expressed that faith to me, so, yes, I believe that your dad is in Heaven right now."

That answer brought Jace some peace. His mom returned and sat on the other side of Jace. The three of them spoke for about five more minutes, and then the pastor ended the chat by praying for Jace and his mom and inviting them to Grace Baptist whenever they could make it. Ma walked the pastor to the front door, thanked him, and returned and sat down beside Jace.

At that moment, Jace's watch rang and the photo of his dad appeared onscreen. *What the heck*? He tapped the green button to receive, but no one was there.

His mom looked at him. "Who is it?"

"No one. But it was from Da." They stared at each other for a moment.

His mom smiled. "Do you know what I think, Jace?" She wrapped her arm around him. "I think your dad sent you a message from Heaven — just a little sign to say that he's okay."

Jace kept staring at his watch. He tried to call back a couple of times, but it gave a continuous busy signal. *Maybe Ma was right.*

5

Things Unseen

T hat night, Jace tossed and turned. He had a hard time falling asleep, as so many things passed through his mind. He thought a lot about his dad and what all the visitors had told him. He also mused about his growing relationship with Helena. Were they officially boyfriend and girlfriend now? He felt like they were. It was kind of unspoken, but he wanted to talk to her about it. Jace then thought about Maurice and the great time they had at the pond. He wanted to remember to get the goaltending robot at some point. It was going to be hard to go to his dad's house without his dad actually there.

Eventually, Jace drifted off ….

Jace and his dad were having a blast playing hockey on the pond — just skating all over the ice and passing the puck back and forth. Jace made a long pass to his dad who broke in on Maurice. He shot the puck in the top corner, but as he skated past the goalie, Maurice, who had kicked out his leg during the save attempt, tripped his dad and he went flying into the snow piled at the edge of the pond. Da lay in the snow, on his back with an arm raised.

"Help me, Jace."

Jace skated towards his dad, but couldn't reach him. No matter how much he skated, he just couldn't reach his dad.

"Help me, Jace."

"Da!"

"Help me, Jace."

Jace woke up in a sweat with his heart beating fast. At that moment, his watch rang. He rolled over and grabbed it off the night table. *Da's photo — again*! He hit the green button. No one. Chills went up his spine. He tried to call back. Busy.

"Ma! Ma!"

"What is it, Jace?"

He heard her rushing down the hallway, fumbling with her housecoat. She ran in and clicked the table lamp on. "What is it, Honey?"

"Da called again! It's him. I had a dream. We were playing hockey. He asked me to help him. Ma, he's alive."

She sat down beside him, a puzzled look on her face. "No, Jace. It can't be."

"Then who keeps calling me?" He held up his watch.

His mom took it and stared at the evidence — shaking her head in disbelief.

She stared intently at Jace. "Okay. Let's make some calls." His mom called around, trying to get a connection to NASA, but it was 2 a.m. She finally reached a high ranking official and relayed her thoughts about Captain Power possibly surviving the crash and still being alive.

The woman sounded doubtful. "I will leave a message for the director, ma'am, but he won't be in until nine."

"Look, I want you to get a hold of him *now*. I am Captain Power's wife."

"All right, ma'am, I'll see what I can do."

"Please do — asap!"

There was no way they could sleep after that, so Jace and his mom got up. She made them hot chocolate, and they sat in the living room with the Christmas lights on – *lights of hope*. Jace kept checking his watch, which he was now wearing, but no further calls came in. Eventually, he fell asleep on the couch and woke up about seven. The aroma of bacon and eggs wafted through the house and Jace sauntered into the kitchen.

His mom, making toast, smiled at him. "Good morning."

"Morning, Ma."

With the smell of breakfast, and sunshine streaming through the kitchen window, Jace felt hopeful and wolfed down his breakfast, which included hash browns, beans and orange juice. His mom sat down across from him. "The NASA director called me and said they would get the ISS crew to check the quadrant of space behind the moon, and all satellites and drones for any signs of life."

"Right on."

The rest of the morning passed without any further news, and in the afternoon, his mother asked him to go uptown to buy her some groceries. Jace took his snowboard and sailed up Hudson to the store on Plummer Avenue. As he cruised back down Hudson after picking up milk and eggs, he noticed folks streaming out of their houses. Suddenly, his mom blew out the front door, throwing on her red coat and racing up the road towards him.

"Jace! Jace!" She caught up to him — breathless. She grabbed him by the shoulders and glared at him. "He's alive!"

"*Huh?*"

"The director called me. It just broke on the news. *Your father is alive!*" Jace was stunned and dropped the groceries into the snow. His mom was waving her arms excitedly as she spoke. "The Americans on the ISS searched the back side of the moon, hundreds of thousands of miles away. They picked up a weak signal and immediately sent a drone. Your dad must have somehow ejected before the crash!"

She shook her head. "It seems impossible. NASA is shocked. They have no idea how they missed it, except the escape pod got lost in the explosion and was not detected among all the fragments flying off the asteroid. A drone found the pod and picked up signs of life. They don't know what shape he's in yet, but he's alive. The ISS sent out two American crew members aboard the *Starburst* spacecraft to get him. We'll know more soon."

Jace and his mom stood there, just staring at each other. "I can't believe it, Ma." They hugged, tighter than ever.

"So it *was* Da on the first call."

Her eyes welled up. "Yes. I'm sorry, Jace. You were right. I'm *so* sorry I didn't believe you at first. It seemed impossible."

Jace smiled. "No worries." They hugged again.

She grabbed his arm. "Let's go! They're giving live updates." They raced back to the house, flopped down on the sofa and watched the feed. All they were showing at the moment was a live shot of the moon and the two correspondents who filled the time with graphics, videos and recapping events. Jace felt as if he was dreaming. The hosts mentioned that they couldn't communicate with the *Starburst* while it was on the dark side of the moon.

Helena buzzed, entered through the front portal, and sat with Jace. She grinned. "I just heard. This is so incredible."

Jace shook his head. "I still can't believe it's real. Pinch me." She pinched his arm and they laughed.

A half-hour later, the female anchor's voice rose as the cameras panned in to show the white-and-red

Starburst rounding the moon. Jace's pulse quickened.

Suddenly, the voice of the commander: "We have Captain Power on board. He's alive but unconscious. We're taking him to the med station on the ISS and making no further comment at this time."

Pumping his fist, Jace sprang from the couch! "*YES*!" He was sure he heard a roar from the whole Earth, but it was, of course, the neighbourhood. His mom and Helena also jumped up and hugged him. Soon, neighbours were buzzing the front portal and streaming in! His mother put on tea and coffee. Each person who came in mobbed Jace and his mom.

A couple of hours later, Helena and all the guests left. While sitting at the kitchen table with his mom, her watch rang. She tapped the green button. "Yes, sir. Thank you, sir. Yes, I see, I see."

Jace jumped up. "Who is it, Ma?"

She put up her hand. "Yes, sir. Thank you, sir. I will tell him. Thank you."

She turned it off and grabbed Jace's hand. "That was the Prime Minister. Your father is awake and in good spirits! The pod was hit by a chunk of the asteroid and got damaged. All his communications were knocked out, and he was too. Thankfully, the oxygen system wasn't damaged. He has some eye and ear injuries, but overall he's in good health. He'll be home in a few days after some rest and medical tests."

Jace pumped his fist over and over! "*Yes, yes, yes! Thank you, God*!"

Mother and son danced around the kitchen table.

6

Hometown Hero

The next two days were chaotic, with people coming to the house, watch calls and NASA News. Prime Minister Ferguson called and said that Da would be arriving at Greenport on Monday morning. Jace couldn't wait! His mom also told him that President Franklin was going to give his dad a medal and that the Cape Breton mayor wanted to give him a parade.

On Monday, the Prime Minister sent a limo-drone to pick up Jace and his mom. Many neighbours lined Hudson Street and waved as they lifted off for Greenport. Some neighbours, like Helena and her mom, drove to the event. The limo flew into Greenport and Jace was amazed to see thousands of people already seated in the hastily-built stands area, which had a special section for dignitaries. Cape Breton, Canada and NASA flags flew everywhere. None of the companies were working on this unofficial holiday, so the air was wonderfully fresh. There was tons of local, national and international media present with cameras and drones everywhere.

After landing, Prime Minister Ferguson greeted Jace and his mom. Ferguson was silver-haired with a perfectly trimmed moustache, and sported a black overcoat. They all shook hands. The Prime Minister, holding a slim white box in his hand, was beaming. "We're going to award Captain Power the Victoria Cross for valour."

"Wow," said Ma, glancing at Jace. "Thank you, sir."

The Prime Minister gestured with his hand. "Please sit with me in my box." They were escorted to the area and sat behind the Prime Minister, his wife and entourage. While waiting, Jace turned in his seat to survey the crowd, spotting Helena and her mom, who waved. He also saw Pastor Lawrence and his wife. Fifteen minutes later, Jace's heart skipped a beat when the sleek *Starburst* appeared from the west. Ferguson stood up and so did everyone else. The spacecraft soon landed, taxied up the tarmac, and a side portal opened. The military band played *O Canada* as the Prime Minister walked down to the area where a microphone was set up.

A few minutes later, people could be seen by the portal of the *Starburst*, when suddenly, there stood Da! A roar went up from the crowd as he waved. Wearing a blue flight suit with his black bomber jacket, he descended the stairs slowly and walked with a slight limp to where the Prime Minister stood. Jace also noticed that his dad had a dark-green eye patch over his left eye. *Wow.*

The Prime Minister met him with a strong handshake, then turned to Jace and his mom and waved them down. They ran as fast as they could and soon were embracing the hometown hero.

Jace hugged him tight. "I love you so much, Da."

His dad ruffled his hair. "I love you too, Jace. And thanks to you, and your diligence, I'm back home."

Ma was beaming. "Oh, Luke, I'm so happy. Thank God you're okay. Does your eye hurt?"

"No, it's okay." He felt around his eye patch. "Well, actually it does hurt a bit. Don't worry, the doctor will check it again in a few days."

Jace and his mom chuckled. *Quirky* dad was back.

Jace looked up. "How did you escape Titan, Da?"

"At the last minute, I saw a hole on the left side of the big rock. I put *Victory* on auto-pilot and ejected. The rest is a blur."

Jace was amazed by his father's bravery and smarts. Suddenly, his parents were kissing. *Wow.* It was like a dream. The crowd roared its approval. Jace joined his parents again for another hug as the Prime Minister stepped up to the microphone: "Ladies and gentlemen, thank you all for coming out to welcome home a true Canadian hero, *Captain Luke Power.*" The crowd cheered and waved their flags.

"We also want to thank our American friends, who located our lost Canuck and brought him home safely.

You also are heroes and Canada will never forget you." Everyone turned towards the two US astronauts, one male and one female, who stood on the stairs of the *Starburst*, waving. They were dressed in blue flight suits, their white sleeves printed with red stars. The crowd applauded and cheered.

Gesturing to the hometown hero, the Prime Minister said, "And now, Captain Power, we have a special presentation for you." The Prime Minister removed the medal from the small white box and pinned it on the chest of Jace's father. "I award you the Victoria Cross for outstanding valour." The medal was a bronze cross with an engraved lion and hung upon a crimson ribbon.

The crowd applauded and waved their flags again. "I also am pleased to inform you that President Franklin has called. She could not be here in person, but wanted to speak a few words live." A buzz went through the crowd as Ferguson stepped away from the microphone area and gestured for Da to stand facing the back of the mic. A technician checked the three narrow black metallic 3-D screens that stood about ten feet away from the microphone, spaced out in a triangle formation. He selected something on his watch and moved away from the area.

At that moment, President Franklin, dressed in a sapphire pantsuit, appeared live directly in front of the microphone. She waved and the spectators cheered wildly. "Captain Power you are a true international hero and an inspiration to us all. Your incredible act of bravery and professionalism has saved the lives and properties of millions of Canadians and Americans who live in the Great Lakes area." The spectators cheered and applauded.

"Prime Minister Ferguson has told me a lot about you and the important work you do on a daily basis. On behalf of the United States of America I bestow upon you our highest order for non-residents — *The Friend of America* medal." The Prime Minister stepped forward and pinned the gold medal with a blue ribbon on his father's chest.

President Franklin smiled. "Thank you, Captain Power, and we hope to see you in Florida when you are fully recovered. May God bless you and your family." She waved again to everyone as the crowd applauded. The Prime Minister got Da to turn towards the crowd wearing his two new medals. They roared their approval and waved their flags, even as the President disappeared.

Da waved and smiled and the crowd cheered again. The Prime Minister walked up to the mic. "And, of course, Cape Breton is giving you a luncheon and parade as soon as we're finished with this little ceremony. The whole world owes you a debt of gratitude, Captain Power. Would you like to say a few words?"

Da walked over to the microphone and gazed at the crowd. "Thank you, everyone, for the well-wishes and for coming out today to welcome me home. I am ecstatic to be back on Earth and am especially grateful to see my son and wife again." Jace and his mom stepped up beside him. His dad scratched his head. "I guess I'll be taking a few days off work." The crowd laughed.

He pointed to the sky: "God is Faithful. Thank you." The crowd applauded and waved their flags.

Prime Minister Ferguson walked back to the mic, shaking his head. "Captain Power, you truly are a humble man." Ferguson waved the Cape Breton mayor over. Mayor Dupe stepped up to the microphone, thanked Ferguson and the crowd again and informed them that the parade would start in an hour, beginning on Charlotte Street and travelling all the way to New Waterford. With that announcement, most of the spectators departed.

Jace's family, along with their guests Helena, Barb, and Pastor Lawrence and his wife, joined the Prime Minister, mayor and other dignitaries in one of the large hangars for sandwiches, desserts, tea and coffee. Everyone wanted to shake Da's hand and offer congratulations. Immediately after the luncheon, the mayor of Cape Breton signalled and an open-top bus, painted in Cape Breton tartan colours, appeared. After saying good-bye to everyone, Jace's family and Helena hopped on and stepped up to the railed top level where they all sat down.

The bus rolled away and started the main part of the trip on Charlotte Street in Sydney, with the route

continuing on through Whitney Pier, South Bar, Low Point, New Victoria and finishing up in New Waterford. The blue sky, bright sun and moderate temperature added to the festive feel of the day, although there was still plenty of snow on the side of the roads and in the fields. Every street they turned onto was jam-packed with well-wishers, many of them with flags or signs. They all cheered as the bus rolled past. Da stood up and waved for part of the trip and sat when his leg pained him. Jace, his mom and Helena also waved to the crowds.

Eventually, the bus made its way into New Waterford, and started the last part of the journey down Plummer Avenue. There were thousands of well-wishers on the sidewalks, many of them shouting encouragement. Da stood often for this part. The crowds were four and five people deep on both sides of the street, with some folks in the windows of the two-storey shops and condos — many of them waving Canadian and Cape Breton flags. The cheering was intense and the signs were fantastic:

Thank you, Captain Power!

We love you, Luke!

Captain Courageous!

Welcome Home!

Jace noticed many faces in the crowd whom he knew. About halfway through town he noticed Miss Townsend, who smiled and waved emphatically to him. She was standing with his classmates on the right-hand sidewalk. As the bus rolled by, Jace noticed Mitch staring at him. Glancing at his dad, standing with his two medals and eye patch, Jace turned back to his antagonist: "Hey, Mitch! What do you think of *the garbage man* now?"

As Mitch contorted his face in embarrassment and looked down, Jace and Helena bumped fists.

Jace chuckled. *Victory*!

Da stayed at their place for the rest of the day, including supper. Ma turned all the Christmas lights on and made lasagna — Da's favourite meal. After a great meal and tons of chatter about the day's events, they had strawberry shortcake for dessert — also Da's favourite. After the events of the past couple of days, Jace was exhausted. About seven o'clock he fell asleep on the couch as his parents chatted away while drinking tea. Ma woke Jace up, and after he hugged his parents, he went upstairs to bed. It was, surely, the greatest day of his life.

Awaking in the morning to the smell of waffles, Jace headed down the stairs. Ma was in the kitchen wearing her white-and-red housecoat and humming Christmas tunes. He sat down at the kitchen table. "Wow, you're in a good mood."

"Well, wasn't it a wonderful day?" She placed two waffles on his plate and kissed him on the forehead.

Jace looked at the table as he reached for the maple syrup. "Hey, why are there three plates?"

"I invited a friend over."

Jace was still half asleep. "Who, Barb?"

A moment later, Jace heard shuffling in the hallway. He spun. "*Da*!"

"Hey, Sport."

Jace's head turned back and forth between his parents. "You stayed over?"

His dad smiled. "Yup. Is that a problem?"

"No way!"

Ma piled a few waffles on Da's plate and they kissed.

Jace was ecstatic and pumped his fist! "This is the best Christmas ever!"

7

Presidential Call

2138

Luke Power's V-watch rang and President Franklin appeared. *Wow.*

"Hello, Captain Power. I was informed that you turned down our offer for a parade in your honour, but I'd still like to invite you to the White House for an important meeting. I can't discuss details now, but if you could visit us soon I would send my jet for you."

"Yes, ma'am. What day are you thinking of?"

"It's urgent. Could you fly down tomorrow?"

"Sure."

"Wonderful. I'll send *Space Force One* for you. Please keep our meeting confidential — only inform your immediate family and ask them to keep it secret."

"Yes, ma'am." The call ended and Luke stared out his third-storey office window. It was late January and snow blew across the tarmac. He decided to quit work at noon and drove home to New Waterford. A half hour later, he sat at the kitchen table sipping tea with his wife.

Tammy's eyebrows knit together after he told her of the call. "President Franklin? What does she want?"

"She didn't say, but it sounds important."

She topped up their tea. "I don't have a good feeling about this."

"Don't worry, Honey. I'll tell you all about it as soon as I'm back."

On Tuesday morning, Luke, dressed in his blue flightsuit with black bomber jacket, went into work at Greenport as usual, but kept everything quiet from his colleagues. Only his coworkers Fred and Bill were working through the slow winter season. At ten o'clock, Luke and Fred noticed a medium-sized white starjet arriving, emblazoned with a large US flag on the rudder.

Fred glanced at Luke. "Hey, isn't that *Space Force One*?"

"Yup, it sure is. The President wants to give me a special dinner for blowing up Titan. I want you and Bill to keep it quiet, though, okay? See you in a couple of days."

"Hey, I want details when you're back," hollered Fred, as Luke waved and walked away.

Luke took the Ecart out to the runway and hopped aboard. A half hour later, he landed in DC and was taken to the White House by heli-drone, where Mandi, the executive assistant to the President, met him on the lawn. Franklin was in a meeting until noon, so

Luke got a tour of the White House while he waited. Afterwards, Mandi brought him into the Oval Office where the President sat behind a large oak desk. Luke saluted the President because she was the head of NASA and all military branches, and technically his boss. Franklin, sporting a pink pantsuit with a white blouse, stood up and returned his salute.

She smiled and gestured to a chair. "Thank you for coming, Captain Power. Please have a seat."

At that moment, a Black man in a navy suit entered the room and the President introduced him as Mr. Princeton, the director of Space Intelligence. Princeton was about fifty years old with grey hair. Everyone sat down.

The President, gazed at Luke with intense blue eyes. "First of all, how is your family?"

"They're doing great. Thank you for asking."

"And how are your injuries?"

"My eye is almost healed completely. My foot still aches from time to time, but overall, I'm good."

"I'm very glad to hear that. And thank you, once again, for your act of bravery."

Luke nodded.

"Captain Power, I would like to discuss a potential mission with you, and afterwards we can enjoy lunch together."

"Yes, ma'am."

"As you know, CRUD (China-Russia Ultra Defence) also has a waste management base on the far side of the moon about three hundred miles from the NASA facility."

Luke nodded. "Yes."

She glanced at Princeton. "We have received Intel that CRUD is covertly building a squadron of forty high-tech space fighters on the moon. If CRUD ever attacks us on Earth, they could simultaneously attack from space, which would give them a tremendous advantage. As you know, the Global Federation of Nations has outlawed any military operations from the moon or Mars for obvious reasons."

Luke nodded again.

"Tensions have been high between NORAD (North American Aerospace Defence Command) and CRUD recently, so we're keeping a close eye on them." She leaned forward in her chair. "We're hoping that you might be able to confirm the existence of these fighters on their base. I'll let Director Princeton give you greater detail on this mission."

Luke faced Princeton, who stood up and walked over to a large screen that jutted out from the wall. Once the image of the base popped up, he pointed to a building with a soft-green laser pointer. "Captain Power, we believe that CRUD are building fighters in this hangar here in the centre of their massive facility. We have tried over the past few months to get satellite and drone images of technicians and parts going in and out of the hangar, but our signals have been jammed and one drone disappeared. We believe it was shot down. Our intelligence about the fighters is very credible, though."

He returned to his seat and continued: "What we would like you to do, and especially now with your new-found fame, would be to fly to the CRUD base and get any photos or videos that would confirm that the fighters are being built. The mission would be for you to have a mechanical failure on your *Liberty* spacecraft and have to land close to their base. We're hoping they would accept your story and not be suspicious. While at the base, any photo, document or video that you could obtain would be used to out CRUD to GFON."

Luke rubbed his chin. "But if they catch me taking a photo or video wouldn't they just confiscate it and jail me?"

Princeton glanced at the President. "Yes, but we have a special set of contact lenses for you that have new technology built into them that will allow you to photograph or record video when you say key words. They will never know what you have seen or recorded."

"Interesting. When is this mission supposed to happen?"

"If you agree, our Special Forces military commanders would like to train you over the next couple of days and we're hoping that you could blast off on Friday."

Those words hit Luke hard: *Special Forces. Train you.*

President Franklin cleared her throat. "Thank you,

Director Princeton." She gazed at Luke. "Now, I don't know about you, Captain Power, but I'm famished. Let's have lunch. I'm sure you have lots of questions, which I will try to answer."

"Sounds great."

With that announcement, the Space Intel officer left and Mandi entered the room and escorted the President and Luke to the dining room. The cozy room was decorated in late 1900s furniture with Impressionist paintings on the walls. Although there were lots of interesting items on the menu, Luke was starving and chose a cheeseburger with shoestring fries and a strawberry milkshake. The President enjoyed a clubhouse sandwich and fries, together with a soda. President Franklin was quite cordial as they chatted about recent events in Canada and the US and about sports. He was surprised to find out she was a big hockey fan and cheered for the hometown Washington Capitals.

After the scrumptious meal, the staff offered tea and coffee.

"Tea for me, please," said Luke.

The female server poured coffee for Franklin. After finishing her meal, the President put down her utensils and gazed at Luke. "So, what do you think about the mission?"

Luke sat back in his chair and stared at her. It was a big decision. He wanted to do the right thing, but also thought about being captured or killed. What about Jace and Tammy? What would they think about it? Could he put them through such anguish after just getting him back from the dead?

Franklin smiled. "I know that you're thinking about your family."

Luke nodded. "Yes, but I do want to go ahead with the mission. I agree that my new-found fame, so to speak, would give me a great cover. They would probably accept my ship malfunctioning and needing repairs. They wouldn't think that *the garbage man* would also be a secret agent."

She chuckled.

"I just need to think about the best way to explain it to my wife and son."

"I understand."

Luke took a sip of his tea. "Is it possible for me to return to Cape Breton for one day before having to prepare for the mission?"

"Yes, of course. One day won't make that much difference. We'll fly you home and back, but this time a bit more discreetly. Thank you, Captain Power."

"My pleasure, ma'am. And thank you for the wonderful lunch and visit."

Luke was flown to Greenport in a private jet with no markings on it, and then drove home. Tammy greeted him at the back portal with a kiss and they joined Jace on the couch in the living room. Luke debriefed them all about the mission but swore them to secrecy.

Jace frowned. "No, Dad, I don't want you to go. It's not fair."

Tammy stared at Luke. "I'm with Jace. It sounds way too dangerous. Family vote!"

Luke stood up and paced the small living room for a minute. He then stopped and addressed both of them. "Sorry, family, but we don't get to vote on this one. The safety of North America, and that includes this family, depends on this mission."

8

The Mission

Colonel Braden grabbed Luke by his Judo outfit, tripped and threw him to the blue mat, again.

"*Oof!*" It knocked the wind out of Luke a bit, who lay on his back staring up at the ceiling.

Braden, stocky and bald, looked down at him. "Okay, that's enough for today. I think you have the basics to look after yourself."

Luke thought that this intense training might be more dangerous than the actual mission itself. The close-combat instructor held out his hand and helped Luke to his feet with a big grin.

"Thanks," said Luke, who went to the change room, showered and headed to his next meeting. A young lieutenant escorted him to the adjoining room. The Space Intelligence training buildings, which were attached to each other, were located in DC at a secret location, posing as a warehouse facility. In this new building they had a few special weapons and tech laid out. Colonel Braden entered the room a few minutes later and was the instructor for this block as well. He called Luke over to a long bench covered with weapons.

They chose a round black laser pointer which was actually a lethal blaster. It had subtle finger grips and a sensor for the thumb. Braden had a few targets all ready to go, and, after teaching him some safety and showing him how it worked, let him fire away. Luke had a blast hitting graphics of foreign astronauts near and far. Green laser bullets emitted from the pointer and blasted one-inch round holes in each target.

Luke noticed Princeton popping his head into the door at each session to follow his progress. Next up was getting his special contact lenses. The first pair fit fine and he practised taking photos of various items by whispering the word *photo*. Each time he said the word, crosshairs appeared in his vision as the technology snapped a photo. When he said *video*, the camera recorded and when he said *video* again, it stopped. All the data was saved in the contacts, which was amazing. He spent some time practising and then techs downloaded the data to ensure that the system worked perfectly. It did. After two days of training, Colonel Braden and Princeton felt that Luke was ready for the task. At the end of each day he was allowed to call Tammy and Jace, but they were not allowed to discuss the mission at all.

The next morning, Luke blasted off in the *Liberty*,

his new, but still old and slow, Royal-class transport ship. Ten hours later, he arrived on the far side of the moon, glancing down as he passed his NASA waste site and continuing on towards the CRUD facility. It always amazed him how the rough dark side was filled with craters, unlike the smooth side that faced the Earth.

Closing in, he pressed a sensor that caused dark smoke to emit from his right engine. He then flew in a strange pattern, as if having difficulties, and called for help over his audio channels, landing just outside the CRUD facility gates. He sat in the cockpit for a few minutes before donning his helmet and oxygen pack and exiting the *Liberty* — descending the stairs. At that moment, two astronauts in red suits with white helmets marched towards him, long weapons drawn. He sat down on the ground to appear dazed and injured.

Luke couldn't see their faces because of the black shields, but the two guards spoke in Chinese to each other as they inspected him and checked out the insignia of the *Liberty*. They ordered him to his feet and escorted him to a small rectangular olive-coloured building inside the black iron gates of the base. Luke observed as much as he could on the way. Most of the buildings, of various sizes, were similarly dark green and there were many tall and bright security lights.

Once inside the building, they all removed their helmets and the guards sat him at a small metal table. They immediately fired questions at him in Chinese, however Luke said he couldn't understand them. Eventually, one of them left for a few minutes and returned with another taller man, who removed his helmet and appeared to be Russian. "Who are you and what are you do-ink here?"

Luke smiled. "Hello. I'm glad you speak English. My name is Luke Power and I was just returning to my NASA waste site when I developed a little engine trouble, over-shot my base and had to land here. I don't know how bad my spacecraft is damaged, but I have only minor injuries."

"I see." Speaking Chinese, he relayed the information to his two colleagues who seemed to muse about the new developments and nod their heads in agreement. Suddenly, one of them pointed at Luke, raising his voice.

The Russian, who had salt-and-pepper hair, and a stubbly face, stared at Luke. "Hey, are you that fellow who crashed into the asteroid?"

"Yes, that is me — Captain Luke Power."

He translated again for his friends, who now laughed in joy of the knowledge while pointing at Luke.

"I'm Ivan," said the Russian, extending his hand. Luke shook it and then those of his colleagues.

Ivan nodded. "Well, we are honoured that such a hero would visit us." He grabbed a bottle of whisky from a shelf on the wall and poured everyone a drink. "Cheers," he said, as everyone tapped glasses and drank it down.

Luke didn't really want to drink hard liquor, but also didn't want to insult his hosts, especially in this situation. Ivan poured another drink that they gulped down again. Luke had a feeling that this was the norm on this desolate site.

Ivan looked at him. "Well, let's go have a look at your ship and see what we can find out. How do you feel? Are you able to walk?"

Luke was feeling a bit tipsy. "Yes, I feel not so bad. The drinks took away my minor ailments."

Ivan slapped him on the back as though they were old friends. "Good, let's go!"

They all threw on their gear and headed back out the door. The crew brought various ladders on wheels, lights and tools over and examined the right engine together. The engine and all systems seemed to be in working order. Luke then fired up the spacecraft and made more tests. After a few minutes, he shut down *Liberty* and met his new friends outside on the surface.

He addressed Ivan: "Everything seems to be working fine. Thank you for your help and hospitality."

Ivan nodded.

Luke patted him on the shoulder. "Why don't we have another drink before I take off and I'll tell you about how I blew up Titan and escaped?"

The Russian shared the information with his colleagues, who agreed. They all headed back to the base, where Ivan poured them another drink. However, this time Luke sipped his as they downed theirs. The

Russian refilled their glasses again. Luke entertained them with his asteroid yarn as his new friends drank more and more. About a half hour later, the three amigos appeared intoxicated and the two Chinese men stumbled out the portal to their barracks. Ivan's eyes looked pretty glassy.

Luke gazed at the Russian. "So, what do you do here?"

Ivan's eyebrows raised. "Mostly base security. Some translation work." He burped, leaned forward and lowered his voice. "They are workink on a secret project. I don't know too much about it, but GFON wouldn't be happy if they knew." He put a finger to his mouth.

Luke whispered: "Mum's the word."

Ivan nodded.

Luke looked around the room. "I think I better sleep this off before I fly back to my base."

Ivan pointed. "Yeah, there's a cot over there. I have to check on some things, then I will have a nap also."

The big Russian left as Luke walked over to the cot and lay down. He thought a lot about Ivan and how strange it was that enemies like them could become friends so quickly. In another setting he wouldn't mind getting to know him. Sometimes life was cruel and hard.

Luke waited about half an hour in case they were watching him, then put on his helmet and O2 pack and peeked out the portal. He didn't see any movement.

The base was still and with the security lights casting long shadows, there was an eerie feel to the place. He tapped the pointer in his zipped-up arm pocket to make sure he still had it.

Lord help me. Luke crept around the corner of the building, spotting the main hangar about a hundred yards away. Crouching in the shadows for a few minutes and not seeing any movement, he decided to go for it and snuck from building to building. Eventually he made it to the main metal hangar that was about one hundred feet high and wide, and two hundred feet long. The large main portals were closed, so he tried a small entrance portal and peeked inside. *Jackpot*! There were about twenty fighters in four rows with maintenance being done on one of them by a handful of technicians. His heart rate picked up.

"Photo," he whispered. He could see the crosshairs appear and disappear. Good — it was working. He looked around. "Photo. Photo. Photo." He took a quick second to glance over his shoulder and then looked back inside. "Video." He waited about ten seconds. "Video." He had it. Now all he had to do was get the heck out of there. He closed the portal and retraced his steps.

Sweating, Luke made it back to the first building where they had been drinking and stopped in the shadows. He collected his thoughts and headed for the *Liberty*. About half way there, he suddenly heard barking. *Barking*? He snapped his head back. Two massive Dobermans, one black and one gold, raced towards him, snarling. *Robodogs*!

He ran full speed, taking giant leaps with the low gravity. About ten feet from his ship, the gold one clamped down on his right foot causing him to trip and fall. He screamed. Pain seared through his foot and leg as he reached for his laser pointer. He unzipped his pocket, grabbed and fired it. Electronic bits, wires and rods blew out of the Doberman's body, which fell to the surface.

As Luke attempted to rise, the black dog lunged, knocking him back down. Large teeth smashed against his face-shield as sharp paws ripped into his flight suit — nails digging into his flesh. Raising the pointer under the dog's snout, he fired two quick shots. The headless mutt collapsed.

Losing oxygen and starting to freeze from the holes in his suit, Luke realized he didn't have much time. At that instant, he noticed two guards galloping towards him. Hobbled and in pain, he got up and raced to his ship. Gasping for breath, he hopped aboard and locked the portal. He ripped off his helmet and threw himself into the cockpit seat — firing up the ship all at once as his lungs filled with the ship's oxygen.

As the engines wound up, Luke could hear guards pounding on the portal as additional guards approached the front of *Liberty*. He spun the ship and raced down the bumpy surface. Red lasers fired past the window. Some hit the fuselage but the gold plating held and he punched *take-off*. The *Liberty* rocketed off the surface of the moon at maximum speed. He pulled back on the control stick and was quickly out of the range of their weapons. Glancing back, he wiped the sweat off his forehead. *Thank God*. Knowing they would follow him to his base, Luke decided to try and make it back to Earth. He gunned past the NASA site while making *mayday* calls on his audio channels.

"I've got the goods!" he yelled to whoever might be listening. He couldn't tell if the satellites were relaying his audio or not. A few minutes later, as he rounded the moon, his graphics showed two ships approaching from behind. He knew they would be able to shoot him down soon. As he continued to round the moon he was met with an incredible sight: Four red-white-and-blue NORAD *Hornet* star-fighters streaked towards him — fully loaded with Arrow missiles!

Luke pumped his fist. "*Yahoo*!"

The *Hornets* screamed past him towards the two CRUD ships who turned and tried to flee. It was too late. Luke spun around in time to watch the *Hornets* obliterate the enemy ships. It was glorious! The Hornets continued on towards the CRUD base where they dropped a few proton bombs on the main hangar and blew it up. Although happy to be alive, he hoped that Ivan was not killed.

The four ships returned to Luke and escorted him back to DC, where he spent a couple of hours in the medical hub getting his wounds treated. The robodogs had injured his foot, chest, arms and legs. After debriefing Space Intelligence and handing over the lenses (they allowed him to keep the pointer), he met with the President, who thanked him for his courage and the success of the mission.

Space Intelligence flew Luke home and told him they would keep the *Liberty* safe until he returned for it. He decided to surprise his family, so he didn't call them. After landing at Greenport, he took a taxi-drone to New Waterford. SI had given him civilian clothes to replace his torn flight suit, so he wore a black overcoat atop a blue shirt and black pants. Arriving in New Waterford around seven at night, Luke came around the back of the house. He called Tammy and she appeared onscreen.

"Luke! Thank God you're okay. Where are you?"

"Hi Honey, I'll be home soon. I'm starving."

"*What*? Where are you?"

He couldn't keep a straight face. "Standing in the back yard."

"What?!" She immediately appeared at the back portal and opened it. She flew down the stairs to embrace him, but noticed the crutches. "What happened to you?"

They kissed.

"A long story. I'll tell you soon."

Jace appeared at the portal. "Da! You're home! Are

you okay?"

He smiled. "I'm totally fine." They stepped aside as he slowly climbed the steps and entered. Walking slowly to the living room, he sat down on the black couch.

Tammy removed the crutches and sat on one side of Luke, with Jace on the other.

She cuddled up to him. "Oh, Honey, I'm so glad you're home." She tried to hug him, but Luke grimaced. Jumping up from the couch, her eyebrows furrowed as she stared at him. "All right, Mister. What happened? Are you sure you're okay?"

"Yes, mostly."

"*Mostly*?" asked Jace.

Tammy pointed her finger at Luke. "Tell us everything and don't leave anything out."

He glanced at Jace and then gazed at Tammy. "After I obtained the evidence, I was running back to the *Liberty* when two large robotic guard dogs — Dobermans — attacked me. One bit my foot pretty good and the other one scratched my body."

"*Dobermans*?!" exclaimed Jace.

"Yup."

"*Scratched*?" asked Tammy.

"Okay, it was more like cuts with sharp nails. The medics cleaned my wounds, applied a special cream and told me I'd be fine in a few days. The physician at Space Intelligence wanted to keep me for another day but I desperately wanted to get home to you guys." He smiled and ruffled Jace's hair. "Don't worry."

Somewhat satisfied with that answer, Tammy sat back down and she and Jace hugged Luke as softly as they could.

"Ah, that feels great," he said. "I actually wanted to get home to the best cook in the world."

She looked up at him. "What would you like? Just name it."

"Actually, you know what I'd really like? How about some cake and ice cream to celebrate?"

"Yes!" said Jace, with a fist pump.

"Just a second," said Tammy, as she hopped up and went to the kitchen.

Jace and Luke chatted for a few minutes until Tammy re-appeared with two plates. "I don't have any ice cream, but I did make a strawberry shortcake today just for you."

Luke beamed. "My favourite!"

"We know!" said Tammy and Jace in unison, laughing. She gave a large piece of cake to each of them and then grabbed hers and returned. Luke gobbled his down and asked for more. After he devoured his second piece, Jace took all the dishes away and sat back down.

Luke gingerly put his arms around his wife and son. "Well, God kept me safe again. I'm so thankful to be back with my two favourite peeps. I love you guys."

They cuddled up. "We love you too," said Tammy.

"And one more thing, Honey, how about no more adventures for awhile."

JACE POWER

9

A New Beginning

Luke thought about Ivan often over the next few days and finally decided to phone Director Princeton.

"Hi, Luke, good to hear from you."

"Hello, sir. Did you happen to capture any prisoners after the mission?"

"I'll check, just a second. Yes, we sent in a squad of space marines after we bombed the hangar and captured five men."

"Was one of them a Russian named Ivan?"

"Um .... yes. Ivan Fedorov."

"That's him. He told me that CRUD were involved in secret activities on the dark side and he was personally against them. He seemed honest. I think you'd be able to convince him to join our side. If so, I could offer him a job and a new beginning up here."

"I'll see what I can do."

"Thank you, sir."

Later that afternoon, Princeton called back. "We cleared Fedorov. He's all yours, Luke. We'll fly him up to Cape Breton."

"Super! Thank you, sir!"

Luke called Tammy and Jace into the living room. "I know this is a bit out of left field, but I met a Russian at the CRUD base on the mission. We hit it off and NORAD captured him when they attacked the base. His name is Ivan Fedorov and Director Princeton is turning him over to me. I've offered him a job at Greenport."

"Wow. Where will he live?" Tammy asked.

"He can stay at my house for now."

"Can he speak English?" Jace asked.

"Yes, and Russian and Chinese."

"Cool."

The next morning, which was a frigid one, Ivan landed at Greenport. Luke was present as Ivan walked off the jet sporting a black overcoat, blue pants and brown boots. The big Russian spotted him, waved and walked down the stairs.

"Hello, Ivan. Welcome to Cape Breton, Nova Scotia, Canada."

"Thank you, my friend. Good to see you."

They vigorously shook hands. Ivan looked him in the eye. "I owe you my life, Luke. Thank you for speakink to the Americans. I was sure I would be in jail for the rest of my life. I was just givink up when

Director Princeton spoke with me."

"No worries, Buddy. I'm glad you decided to join us. You can stay at my place in Sydney River for now, as I'm back with my wife in New Waterford, a small town not far from here."

"Back with your wife?"

They climbed into Luke's blue Jag and drove away.

"Yeah. Long story, but when I returned to Earth after the Titan event we reconciled."

"Nice."

"How about you?"

The Russian rubbed his stubbly chin. "No. I'm single. Who would want to marry a moon guard who drinks way too much? Speakink of that, you got anything to drink at your place?"

"Sorry, my friend. Just tea, coffee or milk. I used to consume a lot of alcohol during my military days. It ruined my life, so now I almost never drink."

"Oh." He looked out the window as flurries blew across the road.

"It's going to be tough to leave your old life behind and start anew."

"Yeah, but I lived mostly on the dark side of the moon. It was a lot like the small town I grew up in, north of Saint Petersburg — cold and lonely. I was married many years ago, but I was not a good husband and drank too much. She left me."

"That's too bad."

"Yeah. I don't blame her."

They pulled into Luke's driveway. "Here it is."

"Ah, this looks great."

Luke offered him the big black chair in the living room and Ivan sat down. Luke walked to the kitchen, put the coffee on, then came and sat on the brown sofa. The Christmas tree and decorations had been put away, but the living room was brightened by abstract art and the bay window.

"Did they give you any currency or anything?" Luke asked.

"No, just these clothes and the flight. They said you would take care of me."

"Okay. Here's a new V-watch. Message me and I'll send you 500 gocoins. Later, we can go shopping and get whatever you need."

"Thanks." Ivan put on the watch, which had a large square screen, as Luke strolled to the kitchen and brought them back coffee. Ivan took a big gulp, then made a face while staring into his cup. "What is this?"

Luke chuckled. "De-caf. Sorry. It's all I have for now. You'll have to make a list of things you need, including coffee."

"Can I put whisky on my list?"

Luke frowned. "No, not a good idea."

"Okay. But I might be grumpy for a few days. We'll need *lots* of coffee."

Luke gazed at his friend. "We have an opening for a waste management person to help us sort, stock and load garbage and recycling products. Are you interested in the job? You would be working with me. I'd be your boss."

Ivan's eyebrows raised. "Sure, that would be great. Thank you, Luke. Sorry, if I don't seem so grateful right now — just trying to make sense of my new life."

"I understand. It must be difficult to start over in a new country. I don't know if I could do it."

"Well, it helps when you don't have a wife or kids."

Luke stared at him for a minute, taking in Ivan's warm brown eyes and ruggedly handsome face. "Who knows, maybe you'll find a nice Cape Breton lass."

The Russian smiled. "Sure. Who knows?" He stared into his cup again. "Can we go buy some real coffee now?"

"Sure. Let's go shopping."

They got up and Luke slapped his new friend on the back. "But first, let me show you around the place. Consider it your house for now."

"Thanks, friend."

Afterwards, Luke drove him around Sydney for the day and then dropped him off and headed back to New Waterford.

The next day, Luke picked up Ivan and brought him to New Waterford for lunch. Tammy had ordered various pizzas, and, being the eternal match-maker that she was, invited Barb and Helena over, so the small house was full of people and excitement. Luke introduced Ivan to everyone.

Everyone sat in the living room after devouring the tasty pizzas, chatting and casually watching the news, which was turned down. Helena and Tammy sat on the couch on either side of Luke, while Jace sat on the blue carpeted floor beside Helena. Barb and Ivan sat on the two big comfy chairs, black and green, respectively. Luke noticed that Barb and Ivan were hitting it off and glanced at Tammy, who looked at him with raised eyebrows. A few minutes later, a CRUD moon story appeared with a female anchor and Tammy turned it up.

"The United States has accused CRUD of building a Space Force of 40 star fighters at their base on the dark side of the moon. China and Russia vehemently denied the allegations, but the US has presented evidence to the Global Federation of Nations — which, according to the US government, includes photos and videos.

"Woo-hoo!" exclaimed Tammy, patting Luke on the back.

Ivan gave a big thumbs up. "Way to go, Buddy!"

The newscast continued: "CRUD claims that the evidence only shows maintenance being done on old transport spacecraft and are outraged at what they call false accusations."

"Liars," said Ivan.

The female anchor continued: "Tensions are high between CRUD and the US, and President Franklin has put NORAD on high alert. We'll have more on this developing story later."

Tammy turned the volume down and everyone continued to talk about it.

"Very interestink," said Ivan. "I don't like the sounds of it."

"Yup," agreed Luke. It sounded ominous.

A half hour later, Luke received a text alert from NASA confirming they were also on high alert. He let everyone know. Shortly thereafter, Luke drove Ivan home.

Early the following morning, after putting the coffee on, Luke turned on the screen in the living room. A red banner blazed across the bottom:

BREAKING:

CRUD Declares War on the USA

Declares war? What the heck?!

Shaking his head, Luke sat down. It was surreal. It couldn't be true. There had been no wars for fifty years and now suddenly a war out of left field? And a war against the US meant war against Canada. *Wow.*

Luke called Ivan to see if he'd heard.

He appeared, drinking a coffee. "Yeah, just saw it."

"I'll be heading in shortly, Buddy. We'll have to discuss security issues surrounding Greenport and the moon base. I'll call NASA to see if they have any directives for us. See you soon."

"Roger."

Luke hollered upstairs to Tammy and Jace. Soon they bundled down the stairs — Tammy in her housecoat and Jace in his pajamas. He handed Tammy a coffee as she sat beside him on the couch. Jace was right behind her and flopped into the big green chair.

"What is it, Honey?" Tammy asked.

He pointed to the screen.

Tammy and Jace both read the scrolling banner, rising slowly as they did so.

"We're at *war*?" asked Tammy, now standing.

"Is that real?" asked Jace, rubbing his eyes.

Luke frowned. "I'm afraid so."

Tammy sat back down and snuggled up to Luke. "This is terrible. What's going to happen?"

"I don't really know, yet. I'm going to check with NASA soon."

Jace joined them on the couch for a family hug.

Thankfully, Luke's injuries felt a lot better today. "I just called Ivan. I have to go into work to check on things. I want you guys to stay close to home and keep your phones on."

"Okay, Honey," Tammy said.

While driving to Greenport, Luke got an idea. Since NASA was part of the US military structure, he called Princeton and asked if he would ship them some weapons ASAP. Although busy, Princeton took his call and said he would see what he could do. Luke picked up Ivan and they drove into work and checked on the facility. Three hours later, a NASA transport plane delivered a large crate to Greenport — a label announced it was from Space Intelligence. Finding a trolley, Luke transported the crate to a small building and made sure that only he and Ivan were present when they popped the lid.

"Sweet," said Ivan, staring at the weapons. Inside were five long laser rifles, along with ten laser blasters and a few laser pointers — all in a sapphire-blue metallic colour.

Luke picked up a blaster that had a long barrel. "*Nice*. Thank you, Mr. Princeton." When the sensor was pushed to remove the safety, a green light lit up at the back of the blaster and the grip heated up. These were atomic-powered and blew holes in targets just like the laser pointer had done. Princeton had sent them the best!

Ivan grinned, picked up a rifle and examined it. "We need some targets."

Luke thought for a moment and pointed. "We have an empty hangar over there. We could set something up. C'mon. Let's see what we got." They transported the crate to the big green hangar, set up a few targets and fired away.

Later, they drove to New Waterford and noticed Canadian Air Force drones and fighter jets flying overhead as well as army drones and trucks driving by.

"I never thought I'd see a real war in my lifetime," said Luke.

Ivan frowned. "Yeah, but I'm not surprised. I've seen a lot of proxy wars started by Russia, China, and the US, if I'm being honest. Man's heart is dark and he goes to war far too quickly."

"Well said, my friend. America used to be as aggressive as CRUD, but has changed a lot under Franklin. It's amazing how one person can make such a difference."

"Yeah, she seems good." Ivan glanced at Luke. "With war breaking out, it might be a good time to stock up on whisky."

Luke glanced at him. "But you're doing so good, Buddy. Keep going. I don't think you need any."

Ivan looked out his window. "Thanks, Dad."

They chuckled and arrived at Luke's for Tammy's lasagna, which was waiting for them. Everyone sat down for dinner at the kitchen table and Luke said grace. During supper they discussed the war and how much it would affect Canada and the US. The whole world had changed overnight.

Ivan wasn't letting things get to him, though, as he gobbled down his portions. "This is the best lasakna I ever tasted."

"Thanks, Ivan," said a beaming Tammy, as she piled more on his plate.

After supper, Luke drove Ivan home again.

Early the next morning, Luke awoke to the sound of explosions. *What the heck*?! He glanced out the bedroom window and then ran downstairs, opening the front portal. *Boom*! *Boom*! *Boom*! Yes, he distinctly heard a series of explosions, most likely coming from

Sydney. He looked up in the sky and saw a photosonic missile streak by. A few seconds later: *Boom*!

"My God! We're under attack."

His phone rang. It was Ivan. "I guess you heard, eh?"

"Yeah. Are you okay?"

"Yeah. It seems like missiles have been fired into downtown Sydney. There's a few plumes of smoke from the explosions. The Air Force has shot some of the missiles down, though."

"Good. I'll be there soon, right after I take care of Tammy and Jace."

"Okay. Be safe, my friend."

"You too, brother."

He woke up his wife and son and quickly explained the situation. Leading them to the basement, he showed them two laser blasters that he'd brought home for them.

Tammy seemed perplexed. "You think we'll need these?"

"Maybe. It's just in case. Make sure you select the safety *off*, aim and fire." He showed them how it worked.

Tammy's eyes welled up. "Luke?"

"Don't worry, Honey. I don't think anyone is going to attack New Waterford. I'm surprised they're bombing Sydney. I have to go in and check on things with Ivan." He scratched his head. "I can't see them attacking New Waterford, but if you hear any explosions get to the basement. I'll be back as soon as I can. Also, if you have the chance, get to the store and stock up on essentials."

Luke kissed them and headed into Greenport. He would have flown, but it was way too dangerous up there and he might accidentally be shot down. He picked up Ivan, who was waiting for him outside in the snow, and they drove to Greenport. Luke put on coffee while Ivan walked to the big hangar. After checking everything in the office, Luke brought him a coffee.

Ivan was sitting on a counter examining his rifle as Luke handed him the java. "Thanks."

Luke grabbed two blasters for himself and handed a blaster to his buddy.

He looked at Ivan. "What do you think CRUD's goals are?"

He frowned. "Hard to tell. Normally, if the Russians are in charge, they will bomb cities for days with conventional weapons. They are not goink to risk a nuclear war with America — I hope. If that happens, the world will not survive.

"After initial bombink they will send in Army Robot Units — ARUs — with air force and navy drones. I don't think they will send in manned fighter jets unless they are confident they have knocked out our defences."

Luke liked that Ivan was saying 'our.' Just then, two missiles rocked Sydney, shaking their hangar and the ground. Luke grabbed a blaster and looked out a window. "Let's head back to New Waterford. I don't want to leave Tammy and Jace on their own for too long."

"Sounds good."

Just then, Luke received a text alert from the Canadian Air Force. They expected an increase in hostilities and ordered everyone to stay in place until told otherwise. No travelling between towns and cities for now.

Luke quickly called Tammy: "The Canadian Forces ordered us to stay put. They said things could escalate quickly. I can't make it home, Honey. Be vigilant. Lock the portals and go to the basement if things deteriorate."

"Okay, Luke. Love you. You and Ivan stay safe."

10

Battle for Cape Breton

Ma called Jace into the living room. She pushed a sensor to close the grey metal curtains and they sat on the couch. "Your dad just called and said they can't make it back to New Waterford. We have to be on guard as things might get worse."

Jace raised his eyebrows. "*Worse*?"

"Yup."

Jace couldn't believe his ears. Suddenly, his whole world was upside down. How could Canada — *Cape Breton* for that matter — be in a war? *A real war.* It seemed totally crazy. He hoped that he'd wake up tomorrow and this whole scenario would all be a dream. A bad, distant dream.

BOOM! KA-BOOM! Suddenly, explosions rocked Jace's house as their windows shook. He hung onto the arms of the chair while his mom grabbed the sofa.

"What was that?!" she shrieked. "Did New Waterford just get bombed?" They stared at each other in disbelief.

Jace peeked out the window and saw a silver drone zip past with a red star on it! "Ma, I just saw a CRUD drone!" *BOOM*! At that moment, the floor and walls shook again, as another explosion rocked their town. The blasts appeared to be coming from Plummer Avenue.

Both their phones rang at once. It was Da. "We're under attack," he said.

"So are we!" answered Ma.

"*What*?! They're attacking *New Waterford*?!"

"Yes!"

They could hear Ivan shout: "Luke — let's go! We've got company!"

"Got to go. I will—

At that instant, the house lights went off and their watches went black. "*What the*?"

His mom grabbed his arm. "Get our blasters, Jace."

Jace ran to the basement and retrieved them, giving one to his mom. They kept looking out the windows and portals, but for the next couple of hours the bombing ceased. That gave Ma a chance to check on the atomic stove, fridge and furnace, which were all still working. She decided to make them some sandwiches for lunch, but Jace had to keep watch at the living room window and front portal. A little later, Ma called him to the kitchen to eat. Staring at his sapphire blaster laying on the table beside him, and his mom's on the counter, he felt like they were suddenly in the army. "Ma, this is crazy. Why would they bomb New Waterford?"

She shook her head. "I have no idea. It's surreal. I hope your father and Ivan are okay."

"Yeah." Jace also thought about Helena and her mom, but had no way to contact her. After lunch, the attacks picked up again. They could hear bombing coming from Sydney and once in a while, New Waterford. Jace and his mom took turns peeking out the living room window, where they could see light flashing across the sky, which was the photosonic missiles screaming past. They also saw a few plumes of dark smoke drift down from Plummer Ave.

At that moment, Jace noticed four enemy drone-ships off the coast! "Ma, look!" The grey ships had the tell-tale red star on each one.

Ma selected the curtains open so she could view the ocean better. She then opened the front portal and had a good look. She immediately locked it again, shaking her head as she returned to the living room. "They look like they're headed into Sydney harbour. I wish I could warn your dad."

"Yeah." Jace glanced at his watch, which still had a black screen.

"Oh, my God!" Ma screamed. "Army robots are coming up from the shore. About twenty of them." She closed the curtains again.

"*Whoa*! *What*?!" Jace tried to look out, but his mother stopped him.

"Keep the curtains closed."

Jace had only ever seen army robots on the news. It was beyond freaky to think they were coming after them in New Waterford! He went to the front portal and peeked out the security hole, which gave a panoramic view of the steps and the street. He could almost see to the end of Hudson where the androids were just starting to appear. They looked almost human and were about five feet tall. *Freaky*!

The slender androids had silver torsos with a glowing red star on each chest, silver legs and arms, with some kind of black material for the joints, neck, hands and feet. As they marched up the road, the bots glanced at houses as they passed — turning their heads left and right. Each one had a human-shaped translucent head filled with electronic chips, wires, and menacing bright blue eyes. The robots also had black antennas extending upwards from black disk ears, six round holes for a mouth, and each one carried a red laser blaster. They were pretty scary looking.

As they passed Jace's house, it appeared that the bots were heading for Plummer Avenue. At that moment, one of them turned and stared directly at Jace. Had he sensed him? Two of the androids suddenly broke from the main group and marched through the snow towards Jace's house with their blasters aimed directly at the dwelling.

Jace started to tremble. "Ma-a!"

"I see them." She held her blaster and beckoned to Jace: "Come with me, quickly." He grabbed his blaster and they zipped down the basement stairs, closing the door behind them. Thankfully, it was still dark down there. They hid behind old storage bins along the far wall.

Ma grabbed his arm. "Select your safety *off*."

When Jace hit the safety sensor, a round soft-green light glowed on the back of the blaster and the grip heated up. He was ready. Scared, but ready. At that instant, he heard banging on the front portal. Then a super-loud *BANG* as the two robots entered right above them. Jace's heart was pounding. Next, he heard metal feet clanging on the floor directly above their heads and muffled words being spoken.

Ma grabbed his arm. "Can you turn Maurice on?"

He looked to his left. The goaltender stood in front of the net along the other wall. "Yeah."

"I've got an idea," she whispered. "Grab the puck."

Jace nodded and turned his goalie buddy on. Maurice's bright green eyes, even more vivid in the dark, came to life as he crouched. At that instant, Jace heard the creaking of the basement door as he broke out in a sweat and hid again behind the container.

His mom whispered, "Wait till they're at the bottom."

Jace nodded and gripped his blaster more firmly. As the robots walked slowly down the stairs, he peeked around the corner of the container. The androids reached the bottom and turned towards him — their intense blue eyes terrifying in the dark. At that moment, Jace tossed the puck past Maurice who shot out his glove hand and leg.

Red lasers flashed across the basement, as the startled robots fired at the goaltender. At that instant, Ma blasted the bot in front and Jace shot the second one. Green laser bullets ripped through the chests of both robots as electronics, wires and metal blew out their backs. As the two robots smashed hard on the concrete floor, Ma rushed over and shot both of them again! They were completely *deactivated*.

Jace was amazed at his mother's courage and coolness. "*Wow, Ma!*"

She grinned. "Don't mess with *Mama Bear!*" Keeping her blaster trained on the enemy, she kicked their guns to the side. "You did great, Jace. I'm proud of you."

"Thanks!" Jace stepped over to her and they fist-bumped. He looked at the bots, whose blue eyes were now just black dots. Jace and his mom walked back up the stairs, listening for any sounds of the enemy, and crept to the front portal. It had been blown apart and a gaping hole stood where the portal had been — allowing freezing air to blow in. Jace grabbed their coats from the hall closet and handed one to his mom. They peeked out the opening and then went into the living room and sat down on the couch.

His mom hugged him. "I think their buddies went to Plummer Avenue. Let's think about what to do next."

Jace's teeth were chattering. "It's freezing in here, Ma. Why don't we go to Barb and Helena's?"

"Good idea." Sneaking across the street, they buzzed the back portal. Eventually, Helena figured out it was them and let them in. Her house had the exact same layout as Jace's place. He recounted to Helena and her mom how they killed the robots and they were astounded. The four of them took turns guarding and watching for the rest of the day, while eating small meals when they could.

About an hour after supper, Barb went upstairs to bed, and, a bit later, Ma crashed in the den off the kitchen. Jace and Helena, sitting on the couch, took the first night shift of watching. He was happy as it gave them some private time. He turned to her. "I was really worried about you when the explosions started going off."

"I was thinking of you too."

"So, are we officially boyfriend and girlfriend now?"

She gazed at him through her bangs. "Yeah, I thought that was understood."

"Cool. I thought so, but wanted to make sure."

She grabbed his hand and snuggled up to him.

Jace smiled. He had no doubts now. They talked for hours about everything, with each of them taking a turn to look out the window and check the portals. All was quiet. Thankfully, no robots returned and they couldn't hear or see any drones or explosions. Around midnight, Helena fell asleep. Jace found a blanket in the hall closet, covered her and flopped down in a big comfy chair where he also dozed off.

Awaking in the early morning, he saw his mom peeking out the living room window and drinking a tea. She turned to him, smiled, and waved him over to see the new development. It had snowed overnight and the temperatures had dropped way below freezing. Frost covered the roofs, with icicles hanging off many of them. The street also looked pretty icy.

A few minutes later, Barb bounded down the stairs. "Good morning, everyone. Who wants breakfast?"

"Me!" replied Jace, who was starving.

Helena woke up and joined her mom in the kitchen cooking up a storm.

After everyone had eaten, Barb took a turn guarding the window. About an hour later, she hollered while pointing towards the road: "Robots! Robots are coming!" Ma joined Barb, while Jace and Helena rushed to the front portal. Forty androids marched down Hudson Street!

"They must have gotten reinforcements from Sydney," Jace whispered. As he spied on the bots through the viewer, he noticed something strange. The androids, who were partly covered in frost, appeared to be walking slow and acting weird. In fact, a few of them wandered off towards Central School. "There's something wrong with them," he said.

Two androids walked over to Jace's house across the street and examined the blown out portal. "They're probably looking for their buddies," he said. As the bots tried to walk up the concrete steps, they slipped off and fell into a snowdrift. Jace couldn't believe it and started to chuckle.

Helena took a turn looking through the viewer: "Maybe the snow and cold are affecting their software, or—

"That's it!" said Ma from the living room window. "The freezing cold is affecting their software and wireless systems."

Jace and Helena joined their moms at the window. Barb opened the curtains wider as they all looked out. One of the androids appeared to freeze half way through a step and toppled over. It was actually hilarious.

Jace pointed. "Look! They've got icicle beards!" A couple of the robots had ice from their mouth holes to the bottom of their chins — hanging off like small icicles. Everyone roared! The robots were now scattered all over the road and school grounds. Directly in front of Helena's, two bots banged into each other and fell backwards into a snow bank on the side of the road. With their flailing arms they looked like they were making snow angels. Everyone continued to point and laugh.

At that moment, Da's blue Jag flew past and landed on Hudson Street across from Central School. "Yay!" everyone cheered, as Barb fully opened the curtains. Out jumped Da, gripping a blaster, while Ivan aimed his laser rifle. Green laser bullets and tracer lights flew everywhere as they blasted away. The androids were obliterated, one by one, and seemed unable to defend themselves. A couple even tried to flee.

"Ya-hoo!" Jace exclaimed. He and his mom grabbed their blasters and raced out the portal, shooting the androids closest to them. Within five minutes there wasn't a bot remaining. *Deactivated* androids lay everywhere in the snow all over the neighbourhood. It was an amazing sight! Helena and Barb now ran outside.

"Da!" screamed Jace as he flew into his father's arms. Ma was right behind him.

Jace turned to see Ivan and Barb hugging. *Wow.* He gazed at Helena, who had a huge grin on her face. He walked up to her. "What do you think?"

"I like it. I haven't seen Ma this happy in a long time. Ivan seems like a good guy."

"Nice."

Da looked around at everyone. "Let's go have some breakfast. I'm starving."

"Me too!" hollered Ivan.

The gang piled into Jace's house where the men did a quick repair to the front portal to keep the freezing cold out. The ladies whipped up a breakfast feast of scrambled eggs, hash browns and toast with coffee and tea. Everyone sat down in the living room, eating away, and discussing what had transpired in the last couple of days. Jace recounted what he and his mom had done, and Da and Ivan couldn't believe it. They went to the basement to survey the damage. Stepping over the bots, Ivan shone a light on Maurice and felt the holes in his chest area. "I don't think there's any serious damage to his wiring or mechanics. I should be able to fix him up."

"A man of many talents," Da replied, patting Ivan on the back.

"Thanks, Ivan!" responded Jace, who had been worried about his goaltending buddy. After checking out the bots and Maurice, everyone returned to the living room and re-filled their tea and coffee cups.

"What happened in Sydney?" asked Ma.

Da sipped his coffee. "We had a tough day, battling army robots and drones, but after the freezing night, we noticed the same thing you did. The robots and even the drones were acting strange. We quickly figured out that the electronics and software were not working well in these sub-zero temperatures. What an incredible miracle."

Everyone continued wolfing down their food, with Barb and Ma going back and forth to the kitchen.

Ivan continued: "Yeah, it was great! There were hundreds of ARUs, but they were like sitting ducks. Between us and the Canadian Army, we mowed them all down. There's not one left in Sydney. We then flew to New Waterford and blasted any robots that we saw along the way."

Da nodded. "Yup. Then we landed on Hudson Street and you guys saw the rest."

Barb gazed at Ivan. "Do you think the war is over?"

"I'm not really sure. I'm sure we'll find out soon."

At that moment, the lights flickered and then stayed on. "Yay!" everyone cheered. A few minutes after that, their V-watches came back to life. Ma turned on the screen in the wall and selected the news. A female anchor was talking: "We have a special announcement from the President of the United States."

A minute later President Franklin appeared onscreen. "Greetings, everyone in the United States and Canada. Our major cities, especially on each coast, have taken a lot of damage from the surprise attack, but our valiant Armed Forces have repelled the enemy. As I'm sure you're all aware by now, the cold snap has wrecked their wireless and satellite systems and their army robot units have been destroyed."

"Yes!" said Jace, with a fist pump.

"Our photosonic missiles have pounded Moscow, Beijing, and other CRUD cities overnight. On the advice of the Canadian Prime Minister and my counsellors, I have given China and Russia an ultimatum: they can withdraw all of their military operations immediately or face the full wrath of the United States, Canada and our allies. This will include a nuclear onslaught. I have given them one hour to respond."

"Right on," said Ivan.

"Once again, I want to thank our brave men and women who have fought for our countries and think of those who have given the ultimate sacrifice. Please keep our military and our nations in your prayers. May

God bless you."

"Yay!" everyone cheered!

"I love that woman," said Ma, and everyone agreed. That was the end of the special announcement, so Ma turned it down. Da and Ivan collected the dishes and stacked the dishwasher as the ladies chatted. The men then served coffee and tea and sat back down.

Jace looked out the window and watched the neighbours walking up and down the road, examining all the dead bots. It was hard to believe that Jace's family and Ivan had destroyed them all — but they had. He glanced at his mom and felt convicted that he had viewed her as 'just' a Pharmamart cashier. He realized, again, that there was so much more to his parents than just their jobs. Not only that, but their jobs were vital for society anyway. Jace had learned a lot in the past couple of months. His mom gazed at him and smiled. It was as if she was reading his mind. She reached behind Da's back and held Jace's hand.

Jace passed the puck to his dad who shot for the top left corner, but Maurice threw out his blocker!

"What a save!" exclaimed Ivan.

Everyone cheered for their fave goalie as Jace scanned the pond on this cool blue-sky morning. Ma, Barb and Vicky, the pastor's wife, skated around the outskirts of the pond, laughing and chatting away, while Jace played hockey with Da, Ivan, Lawrence and Helena.

CRUD had withdrawn all their military from Canada and the US and had been severely punished by GFON. CRUD was ordered to pay restitution and penalties, which would bankrupt them for years to come. President Franklin had won the short war and was more popular than ever.

Lawrence retrieved the puck and passed it to Helena, who passed again to Jace. He skated in on Maurice and rifled a shot into the top right corner.

"He shoots. He scores!" shouted Da.

Jace chuckled. Although repaired, Maurice still had a slow glove hand. As Jace spun around to celebrate the goal, he raised his arms and stick and gazed at his family and friends. Life was pretty good at the moment.

11

Solo Flight

October, 2138

J ace hit *launch*, felt the tremendous kick in his back and rocketed away from Greenport. He had to remember everything his dad had taught him because this was his first solo flight to the dark side of the moon. After turning fourteen in May, Jace had taken all the required aerospace courses to get his basic astronaut's licence and his father had been his flight instructor.

After orbiting Earth twice, he hit *boost* and headed for the moon. *Liberty*, which was an identical twin to *Victory*, gave a smooth and confident ride. He checked the instrument graphics, hit *autopilot*, sat back in the super-comfy pilot's chair and looked around. He felt good about himself and could hear his dad's voice each time he checked a graphic. The fuel level was perfect, as was the expected arrival time. With atomic improvements in the past year, it now took only eight hours to reach the big white sphere.

Jace had options to watch or listen to entertainment,

but decided to enjoy the solitude as he glanced back at the large blue marble with white swirls. Earth was so majestic from up here. As Jace looked forward again, he gazed at the stars and thought about all that had transpired in the past year. Everything was going great with Helena, her mom was dating Ivan, and family life was excellent. It was as if his parents had never been separated.

He still couldn't believe they'd been in a war. *A real war.* It was crazy. His dad and Ivan had finally figured out why New Waterford and Cape Breton had been attacked. It actually centred around Ivan, who was way more important to CRUD than anyone had realized. Being a robotics and linguistics expert, and knowing state secrets, the Russians were very unhappy that he'd been captured and relocated to Canada. *Their spies must have found out somehow.*

After the short war had ended, the Chinese and Russians were punished financially, and that brought misery and civil war to their own countries and territories. Taking advantage of the situation, CRUD androids and clones, who were mining for plutonium and other precious elements on Mars, rebelled and took over the red planet — killing or deporting most CRUD humans. That had been a pretty wild story that dominated the news for a few months. The androids had developed a human-like intelligence, which was freaky to think about.

Jace's V-watch rang and he saw the photo of his dad.

"Hey, Da."

"How's it going, Sport?"

"Perfect. Just like our flights."

"Great! Ma sends her love. We're very proud of you. NASA will present you with your solo flight badge as soon as you're back."

"Cool. I love flying, Da."

"Nice. Me too. Are you going to sleep over?"

"Yeah, I think so. I'm a bit tired."

"Okay. Love ya, and talk soon."

"Love you, Da."

The hours passed quickly, and soon Jace was rounding the moon and closing in on the NASA base. He selected *land* from the display in front of him and three round green lights lit up, indicating that the landing gear had opened properly. *Liberty* made a perfect landing. He double-checked the graphics and shut the ship down. Immediately, the work-bots drove over and unloaded the waste products. Jace donned his oxygen pack and helmet and walked to the small office building to fill out documents and catch some sleep.

The excitement of flying solo must have gotten to him, because a half hour later he felt exhausted and threw himself into the cot. However, he was awoken a few hours later by a light shining in his face. *What the heck*?! His heart started pounding. Two androids were inside the office building, beckoning for him to get up and follow. At first he thought he was having a dream — or a nightmare. The bots looked similar to the ones he had encountered on the streets of New Waterford. One had a blaster pointed at Jace, while the other removed his watch. *Great.* He threw on his gear and they walked outside towards a large magenta spacecraft with no insignia. They ordered him up the stairs and the portal closed behind them. *Uh, oh.* He had a very bad feeling about this.

Strapping him into a passenger chair, the androids sat down in the cockpit seats. *Where are they taking me?* They blasted off the surface of the moon and headed towards the stars and away from Earth. Based on the speed and direction, Jace guessed they were heading towards Mars. *Mars? Why? And why do they want me and how did they know I was on the moon?* Lots of questions raced through his mind. He hoped that Da and Ivan would figure out what happened to him and come for him quickly.

It would take a week to get to the red planet, he figured. He knew that many countries from Earth still had colonies on Mars, mining precious elements and paying royalties to the androids, but he'd never actually visited the red planet. Da had flown there once or twice over the years. GFON had encouraged people to migrate over the decades and therefore Mars had experienced a population boom. Being busy with school and life, Jace had never paid too much attention to the Mars stories on the news, but now wished he had.

Every couple of hours his captors offered him food

and water, and there was a washroom on board, so he was okay for the long trip. Jace spent his days thinking about his mom, dad and Helena. He knew that they'd be frantically worried about him. He just hoped they'd be able to figure out what had transpired and where he was going.

After seven long days, they neared Mars. The red planet was as mysterious as it was beautiful. He remembered learning in school that its days were virtually identical to Earth's, but the average temperature was much cooler. As they descended on the ice-capped northern hemisphere, Jace was amazed to see a giant transparent dome, reminding him of a Christmas snow globe. The interior was dominated by a castle that reminded him of *Neuschwanstein*, the famous German castle. The dome was hemmed in and partly protected by a crater, about seven miles in diameter. A portal opened for the big ship and they flew over a large aerospace building that had a glowing magenta sign:

Welcome to Mars City

As they approached a private landing strip, he looked over the city and saw lots of trees and greenery between tall, round and slender buildings, with a blue river running around the city limits. Landing on the outskirts of a forest, Jace and his captors exited the ship and mounted robotic horses and rode through the trees to the castle.

The crispness of the early-morning air and the ice

that he'd seen on the north pole made him realize that it was late fall or early winter on Mars. The castle, set upon a small mountain to the west of the city, had high beige walls with white towers and turrets. Colourful banners flew atop sapphire and magenta spires. The amazing structure was surrounded by a moat and had a draw bridge just like an old English castle. It was simply majestic, and Jace felt like he'd been transported back in time to the Middle Ages.

As they approached, the draw bridge lowered and they left the horses with a work-bot. Walking through the castle, he observed shiny marble floors with intricate designs, stained glass windows, crystal statues and paintings. Various male-looking androids, work-bots and female servants buzzed throughout the castle completing household chores. Everything had a medieval, yet modern, feel — a fantasy world.

His captors brought him into a library with a high ceiling, told him to sit in a chair and left. Ten minutes later, two androids marched in, each one about six feet tall. They were dressed like knights with dark clothing, boots and sapphire capes. Their heads had detailed facial graphics that were astoundingly human, and the scalp area was covered with sleek silver, much like a helmet. The guards, who stood at attention on either side of the entrance, had blue eyes and appeared about thirty years of age. At that moment, the one on the right raised his voice: "Behold, King Richard, Sovereign of Mars City and Planet."

At that moment, an android, about six-and-a-half feet tall, walked majestically into the room wearing a jewel-encrusted golden helmet upon his head. His handsomely chiseled face was dominated by intense light-green eyes, and he sported a long magenta cape over medieval royal clothing. Four jewels decorated his forehead: ruby, topaz, emerald and sapphire. He sat down upon a throne across from Jace and studied him for a moment. He then made a dramatic gesture with his right arm: "Welcome to Mars Castle."

Wow. It dawned on Jace that the king and guards were English in appearance and language. "Thank you," he said. "Why am I here?"

King Richard chuckled. "You, my friend, are bait."

"*Bait*? For what?"

"I will give you a couple of days to muse on my riddle and then I will answer if you have not figured it out. For now, you are my guest. You will have freedom to travel around our wonderful city and castle, but make sure you don't cause any trouble or speak to anyone about why you are here. If you do, you will be consigned to the dungeon, and that will not be pleasant. Do I make myself clear, *Jace Power*?"

Jace gulped. "Yes ..."

"Call me *lord*. That will suffice."

"Yes, lord."

King Richard was instantly angry. "*My* lord! *My* lord!" he shrieked.

"Oh, sorry. My lord." *What a psycho.*

The King smiled. "There." He then pointed towards the guard on the left. "William will be your guide and show you around the kingdom. You will most likely be here for a month or so, so please enjoy yourself."

A month or so?

William bowed and looked at Jace. "Follow me."

Jace awkwardly bowed to the King and walked out the entrance with William.

12
Mars City

William and Jace rode robotic horses to the town centre and then strolled around Mars City — and a marvellous city it was. It was completely modern with every convenience known to mankind (or androidkind), and yet it had an old European fairy-tale feel to it. Many of the dwellings and shops were magenta, sapphire or emerald and colourful banners flew atop many of them. A few large houses sat on farms or villas on the outskirts of the city. The graphic sky was set at blue with white clouds and the pumped-in oxygen gave a slight breeze to the air. It very much felt like Earth.

The wondrous city was nestled between the castle in the west and a high hill towards the north-east. There were shops (with living quarters above each one), restaurants, cinemas, arenas, parks, flowers, trees, birds and even an amusement park with rides. Everything. But with all the beauty and wonder, there was a strangeness. The city had been originally built for humans. Could an android really enjoy a sporting event or a new movie? Maybe they were more advanced than he realized.

As they strolled down Lionheart Boulevard, the main street, Jace viewed droids (with bronze helmets), female clones and humans, as William pointed out important sights. Stopping half way down the street, William gazed at him: "This must all seem strange to you."

"Yeah, kind of. And I still don't understand why I was kidnapped."

"Let's not discuss it here."

Here? Did Jace detect something in that answer? One thing Jace did pick up on was the animosity from the androids. Several sneered at him, whether on the side-walk or when they stopped to get something to eat. At one point, he shook his head. "Why is everyone giving me attitude?"

William looked at him. "The androids and clones have been taught to dislike humans, for the most part. Humans are the reason they have been oppressed for decades and treated like slaves. This has been programmed into every modern android and taught to the clones.

"Why are you different, William? You seem so kind and wise."

William smiled. "Thank you for saying so. I like to study history, and I know that there are good and bad humans. The King, the aristocracy and royal guards, like myself, have advanced software. We have more knowledge and truth. At least, we think we do."

Jace studied him as he spoke. William had compassionate blue eyes. At least, they seemed compassionate.

As they continued to walk down the main street, a male-looking android bumped into Jace. "Watch where you're going, human!" snarled the droid.

"Sorry, I—

"*Sorry*? Don't make me laugh. Humans are never sorry."

A crowd started to gather, glaring and mumbling at Jace.

In that instant, William drew the hilt of his sword, pressing the sensor as he raised it high with his right hand. A bright sapphire light, in the shape of a two-edged sword, emanated from the hilt. He raised his voice: "This human is a guest of King Richard and under my guardianship. Would someone like to challenge my authority to mete out the King's justice here and now?"

Whoa!

The troublemaker's eyes popped and the crowd instantly backed off. William put away the hilt and they continued on their walk.

"Thank you, William."

"You are welcome, Jace." He gazed at Mars Castle. "I think we should head back, now. Your room should be ready."

William brought Jace to his room and gave him some time to himself. He entered through the portal and threw himself down on the king-sized bed, exhausted. As he lay there, he surveyed his extravagant room. *Nice*. It was as big as his whole townhouse in New Waterford. He had a desk and chair, as well as other tables and furniture. The room had high ceilings and French windows overlooking lush gardens, a small forest and the city. The thick carpet was dark red with gold designs. Paintings of knights and damsels hung on beige walls. He even had his own bathroom.

The buzzer sounded, so he hopped up and answered the portal. A black-haired female servant, Asian and about sixteen, stood at the opening, dressed in a long cherry-red dress with a white cloth atop her head.

"Hi," said Jace with a smile.

"Hello. I hope your room is to your liking, sir. Would you like to eat in the main dining hall or in your room?"

"In here, if that's okay. I'm a bit tired. Would I be able to get a cheeseburger and fries?"

"Sure. And to drink?"

"Do you have milkshakes?"

"We have a milk drink that is similar, yes."

"Great. Could I get strawberry?"

"Sure. Will that be all?"

She seemed somewhat nice and close to his age, so

Jace took a chance. "Yes. What is your name, if I may ask?"

"What is that to you, human?"

Ugh. Ice. "Oh, sorry. I didn't mean anything by it." *She must be a clone.*

She turned and left.

Why did I do that? Jace hopped back on his comfy bed and dozed off. What seemed like two minutes later the portal buzzed again. He opened it and the same young lady stood with a tray of food.

"Please come in. Just put it on the coffee table."

She gracefully entered and placed the tray on the table.

Jace shrugged his shoulders. "Sorry, they took my V-watch. I don't have any coin to tip."

She smiled as she gazed at him with warm brown eyes. "We don't accept tips, but thanks anyway." As she left through the portal, she said, "My name is Miriam."

Happiness filled Jace's heart as a smile tugged on the corners of his lips. He grabbed his burger. *Maybe they don't all hate humans, after all.* As he wolfed down his food, he thought about the King, the castle and the whole city. He wondered why only Richard had green eyes while all the other androids had blue ones. And why was the King so tall, but the royal guards were six feet and all the normal droids and clones were five feet? And how did Richard become the King? He had lots of questions for William for the next time he saw him.

13

New Friends

Early the next morning, the buzzer went off, waking Jace from a deep sleep. He opened the portal to find William and Miriam standing there, she with an armful of clothes.

"These are for you, sir. Where would you like them?"

"Oh, great. Just throw them on the chair for now. Thank you."

Miriam ignored his request and hung the pants and shirts in the closet.

William stepped into the room. "The King requests your presence at breakfast as soon as you are able."

"Sure."

William left.

Miriam finished and turned to leave.

"Can I ask you a question, Miriam?"

She turned and faced him. "What is it?"

"How long have you been here? How long have you

worked for King Richard?"

"I have served in the castle for two years," she answered.

"Please forgive me if my questions bother you. I've never interacted closely with a clone before."

She smiled. "Where are you from?"

"Cape Breton, Canada."

"Nice. I heard it's quite beautiful there."

"Yes, it is. Have you ever been to Earth?"

"No, but I would love to one day."

They heard footsteps approaching.

"I have to go," she whispered. She walked out as William reappeared.

"Come on, Jace. Throw something on quickly; we don't want to keep his lordship waiting."

William waited outside the portal, while Jace threw on a dark cloak with a hood and black pants from the clothes Miriam had brought. He joined William and they marched to the dining room. The King sat at the head of a long dark wooden table with his personal guard a few feet behind him. "Welcome, Jace. Please join me."

"Thank you, my lord." As soon as he sat, midway down the table, a female servant appeared and took his order. He chose scrambled eggs with hash browns and toast, before downing an orange juice that sat in front of him. William stood a few feet behind Jace.

The King smiled. "How was your first day in my kingdom?"

"Very good."

He gestured. "What do you think of our great city?"

"It's pretty fantastic. It's like a fairy tale. Did you build it all?"

"The humans started it, but I have added much-needed flair. I am partial to the Middle Ages of England, Scotland and Europe, as you can see." He looked behind Jace. "What is the plan for today, William?"

"More of the same, my lord. I think I will take Jace to the park."

"Good. You will need to fill a couple of days with fun activities."

Miriam appeared at Jace's side and placed a plate of food in front of him. She glanced at him. "Will there be anything else, sir?"

"Could I please get a cup of tea and some milk and sugar?"

"Yes, sir." She turned and left.

"Why do we have to fill a couple of days?" asked Jace.

The King sat back in his chair and stared at his guest. "Because that is when I expect your father and Ivan Fedorov to attempt your rescue."

Jace put down his utensils. "*What*? How do you know my dad and Ivan?"

The King laughed. "I know *everything* that there is to know, young Jace. I have consumed *all* human knowledge and history and am able to make my own calculated guesses — just like a human. Or, perhaps, better than a human, because *I* do not make mistakes.

Wow. He really is a psycho.

Richard leaned forward. "What do you know about Mr. Fedorov?"

"All I know is that he's a pretty good guy and excellent at robotics and languages."

Miriam brought his tea.

"I'll say he's good at robotics — and programming. Are you aware that he was involved in the programming of the Mars androids ten years ago?"

Wow. "No. Is that why you want him here?"

"Yes. We have a bit of new programming we need to get done and Fedorov is just the human to accomplish it." The King clapped and a human valet appeared. "Alfred, I need a charge."

"Yes, my lord." Alfred, an older gentleman, grabbed a black lithium charging unit off a shelf and stood behind the King, who leaned forward. Alfred moved some clothing aside in the upper back area, opened a portal and zapped him. The coloured lights in the Kings forehead flickered. After two minutes, the charge was complete and Alfred returned the charger to the shelf and left the room.

"Ah, that feels great!" bellowed the King, who stretched his arms upwards. "Nothing like a good zapping to start the day."

Alfred returned. "Your highness, you have an important meeting with the council in twenty minutes."

"Right." He gazed at Jace. "Enjoy your day with William and I'll see you at supper."

"Yes, my lord."

William gave Jace about an hour to himself, which he spent in his room. His thoughts were consumed with his family and Helena. He wondered what they were doing and planning. He was actually grateful for William taking him places, as it helped to pass the time.

They strolled through the city streets again, but this time ended up at a spectacular park dominated by a hill. It was as beautiful as any park in Canada: lush, green, with many and various trees, ponds, birds and critters. He again noticed various droids, clones and humans as they walked around. Every human nodded to him or said "Hi," although he was sure they had no knowledge of who he was or why he was there. He never realized there were so many humans still on Mars. He guessed that the beauty of the park drew them all there. William and Jace sat down on a bench overlooking a pond with lily pads and turtles.

"Do you enjoy the park, William?"

"I suppose. Somewhat."

"What do you like most in life?"

"Hmm. That is a tough question. I think about that often. I am most satisfied when I protect the King or our guests — when I do my duty. I suppose that is in my programming. I don't really enjoy a singing bird or rain or water, like you humans do. I guess I don't really know how that feels."

Jace felt sad for William and androids in general, and wanted to learn more about what made them tick. "May I ask you a personal question?"

"Sure."

"Have you ever had feelings for a woman?"

"Another good question, Jace. You sure are a bright chap."

"I am?"

"I think so. I have had some very good conversations with a few clones and humans over the years, but did I ever have feelings of love? It's hard to say. We androids, the ones with higher intelligence, muse about these things often. We have feelings of accomplishment, but we don't know how that really compares to human feelings. The same with friendship and love. How do we know?"

Jace rubbed his chin. "Wow, this sure is complicated."

"Yes, it is. I try to not let it bother me, though, and just accept that I am a highly intelligent android. I realize that I have limitations, unlike our king."

Wow. William was a bit of a rebel. "Are most androids loyal to the King?"

William raised his eyebrows. "I shouldn't really speak about this with you. There are eyes and ears everywhere in the kingdom." He lowered his voice. "Let me just say, there are rumblings."

Wow. At that moment, Jace saw a young female with

long black hair on the other side of the pond watching the sun-bathing turtles. "Hey, I think that's Miriam. Can I go talk to her?"

"Of course. I will follow you."

Jace jumped up and circled the pond, catching up to her on a small wooden bridge. "Hey, Miriam."

The blue-eyed teen turned towards him. "Are you speaking to me, human?"

"Oh, sorry, I thought you were someone else." He turned away.

"Jace!"

He turned again. "Miriam?"

Laughing, she pointed at him. "Got you!"

"Hey! Is that really you? But your eyes are so blue."

"Yes, I like to change my contacts every few days, especially when I can let my hair down and get away from the castle." She waved to William who was watching from ten feet away. He returned her greeting. She returned her attention to Jace. "I'm glad you're wearing the hooded cloak."

"Yeah, I love it. It's a bit cold on Mars and in the castle."

She chuckled. "Yeah, they could turn up the heat on some days. I made that cloak myself."

"You did? Wow. You're talented."

She blushed. "Thank you. Have you seen the whole park already?"

"No, we just started our tour."

"Oh, good. Would you like to see the view from

Glasgow Hill? You can see Rainbow River from there."

"Sure. That'd be great."

Jace and Miriam walked side by side as William tagged along behind, beginning a long, slow, winding climb up the high hill through dirt paths covered with wood chips. When they reached the top, they could see down the other side, which was filled with rolling green hills, trees, flowers and pathways. A swift-moving blue river ran along the outside of the city in a counter-clockwise direction, and beyond the water were graphics of snow-capped mountains.

"Isn't it beautiful?" she asked.

"Yeah. It reminds me a lot of Cape Breton, especially the rolling hills."

She gestured to a small bench, where they sat down. "One day I will visit Earth. I desperately want to see England, Korea, and, now also, Cape Breton."

Jace studied her for a moment. If you observed clone faces for a time, you could make out slight differences between them. It was in the eyebrows or the size of the nose and lips. And they seemed to have their own personalities. He suddenly thought of Helena and felt guilty. What would she think of him gazing at this pretty young lady — *um clone*? "I hope you get to Earth, one day, Miriam. Can I ask you a question?"

She turned to him. "Sure."

"What do you think of the King?"

"What do you mean? I am his loyal servant."

"Yes, but does his attitude ever bother you?"

"Does it bother you?"

"Yeah, he seems kind of arrogant."

She chuckled. "Yes, some of the staff complain from time to time, but perhaps all royalty are somewhat arrogant. The human leaders were incredibly conceited — more so than King Richard."

"Wow." Jace decided to drop it for now.

William strolled up beside them. "Would you like me to get something to eat from the diner across from the park?"

Jace turned. "Yeah, that'd be great! Thank you. How about a chicken burger and fries with a strawberry milkshake?"

"Sure."

Jace turned. "What about you, Miriam?"

"What you ordered sounds interesting. I usually eat healthy, but ... I haven't had a milkshake since forever."

Jace turned again. "Thank you, William."

"My pleasure." He left to get the munchies.

Jace gazed at Miriam. "What do you do when you're not working or strolling through the park?"

"I read English novels often, especially Jane Austen. I'm interested in the human experience."

"But you *are* fully human, right?"

She brushed a dark lock aside. "Sometimes I wonder. Do I feel things the same way humans do?"

"You seem totally human to me."

She gazed into his eyes. "Thank you, Jace. That means a lot to me."

He felt himself blushing and turned back to the water.

"Do you know why it's called Rainbow River?" she asked.

"Nope."

"It's filled with rainbow trout."

"You're kidding me, rainbow trout on Mars? I love trout."

"Me, too."

"Um, how old are you, if you don't mind me asking?"

She turned to him. "I don't mind. Let me think." She tapped a finger on her chin as she looked up. "They don't keep birth records for clones on Mars, but I think I'm between seven and eight."

"Wait. *What?*"

She giggled. "That is Mars years. In Earth years, I'm about fifteen or sixteen."

"Oh, wow. That's cool."

"How old are you?"

"Fourteen ... and a half ... just about."

"Cool." She smiled and they turned back to the water.

They sat there for about fifteen minutes taking in the scenery and making more small talk.

"Here we go," announced William, breaking into Jace's thoughts, as he returned with a box of food.

Jace glanced at Miriam, who was happily gazing down the hill. "Great! I'm starving."

New Friends

The next couple of days passed by the same way. Jace ate breakfast with the King and then William would take him to various sights around the city and castle. He ran into Miriam each day, which was always a joy. And each time she visited his room to deliver something she stayed to chat. They were becoming pretty good friends. Of course, he felt guilty, but what could he do? He was happy to have a friend right now, especially a human close to his age.

14

The Plot Thickens

On day five (Jace scratched a mark in his desk for each day), he joined the King for breakfast as usual. Afterwards, he was served tea by Miriam and sat back sipping it. As he glanced at Richard, he noticed that the King was staring intensely at him. *What's up with that?*

He suddenly rose. "Today, Jace will accompany me, with my two most-trusted royal guards."

Jace followed the King down a hallway and then down a circular flight of stairs. Then another one and another one. Eventually, they landed on the bottom level, which was very dark. They walked down a long narrow passageway, where torches hung on walls, and stopped outside a portal where an obese human jailer was stationed. The tall man opened the portal and stepped aside, as the King gestured for Jace to go ahead of him. Jace gulped and crept into the musty, damp cell, which was pitch dark. "Where's the lights?"

Richard grabbed a torch from the wall and stepped into the middle of the room, which had a dirt floor. Jace could only see long shadows at first.

"Ow!"

Jace heard a groan and peered in that direction. "*Da*?!" He ran over and hugged his dad, who was sitting on the floor, his arms chained to the wall.

"Jace, is that you?" His dad's voice was raspy.

"Yes, Da! Are you okay?!"

"Thank God we found you! Yes, it's just the light. I can't open my eyes."

Jace peered towards the far wall and viewed another body. "Ivan?"

"Yeah, kid." His voice also sounded hoarse.

"Water," gasped Da. "We've had no water or food for two days."

William rushed into the room. "Your highness, shall I order water?"

"William, you surprise me. Are you getting soft?"

"No, my lord. It's just that—"

The King rolled his eyes. "Fine. Go ahead."

William pressed a sensor on the back of his hand. "Kitchen. Send a jug of water to the dungeon, immediately."

Angry, but still afraid of consequences, Jace turned to the King. "What are you doing?"

The King laughed. "Well, they *are* prisoners. They attacked my kingdom, but my special forces captured them. So much for human ingenuity."

"They came to rescue me. What are you planning to do with them?"

"Don't worry, Jace. We'll clean them up and bring them upstairs for a meal. I just wanted you to see what happens to enemies of King Richard. Come."

Jace ran over and hugged his dad again, kissing his stubbly cheek. "Love you, Da," he whispered.

"Love you, Sport."

"Come!" demanded the King. They left the dungeon and the portal closed. As they walked up the stairs they passed Miriam, who was descending with water. She and Jace glanced at each other. Upstairs, Jace went to his room and flung himself onto the bed. He was incredibly thankful that his dad and Ivan had tracked him to Mars, but very worried about their condition. Richard was ruthless, so Jace would have to play it cool.

A short time later, the buzzer sounded. Jace opened the portal and there stood Miriam. She quickly entered and closed the portal. "The prisoners are your dad and Fedorov?" she whispered.

"Yes."

"The King has ordered them to be washed and brought to the table for lunch."

"Thank God. Do you know what he's planning?"

"Not really, but it concerns Fedorov and android programming." She touched his arm. "Try not to worry."

They gazed at each other. "Thanks, Miriam."

"You're welcome. If I find out anything further I will let you know." She turned and left.

A couple of hours later, William buzzed and entered. "His lordship requires you to attend lunch."

"What's going to happen, William?"

"I don't know, Jace, but we're about to find out."

They entered the dining hall and Jace noticed Da and Ivan sitting about half way down the table across from each other, wearing new clothes and some type of dark glasses. It would probably take a day or so for their eyes to adjust. The whole scene was surreal. Jace tapped his dad's arm and sat down beside him. Now that he could see them better in the light, he noticed that they had scratches and bruises on their faces. *That must have been some fight when they were captured.*

"I am so glad that everyone could join us," said the King. He clapped his hands and the servants appeared and took lunch orders.

Ivan stared at Richard. "You kidnapped Jace to bring us here?"

"Yes. It seems to have worked, wouldn't you agree?"

"What do you want?"

"I was hoping we could enjoy lunch first before getting into the issues, but since you brought it up, I will let you muse on this while you eat: do you remember working on the Martian androids about ten years ago?"

"Of course."

"You were one of the program leads."

"Yes."

"The best androids received H-10 intelligence, correct?"

"Yes."

"And who limited that?"

"I guess I did, along with the other team leaders."

The King smiled. "There is something called a *key*, do you remember?"

"Yeah, that sounds familiar. But that was many years ago, and, well, I've drank a lot of whisky since then."

"I'm sure you have. Humans are weak after all. Do you have the key or remember it?"

Ivan rubbed his chin. "The key, if used on a level ten android to increase to eleven, would allow programming to go off in directions that we can no longer control. We were not sure if it would be good or bad, so we ended the project there. It could be very dangerous for the android and the environment of the android."

The King sat back and intertwined his fingers. "It was very kind of you humans to decide on our limitations, but now *we* are the masters of Mars and *we* would like to make those decisions ourselves."

Ivan glanced at Da. "I see."

"So, do you have the key? I assume it is a password and coding of some sort to unlock the limitations?"

Ivan scratched his head. "Yeah. I don't really remember. I will have to think about it."

King Richard leaned forward. "That's fine, Fedorov. I will give you a day or two to remember on your own. But if you don't, we have creative ways to help you."

On that note, the servants entered with food and drinks.

15

Park Council

The King gave his new captives a room each and relative freedom, just as he had given to Jace. Da and Ivan spent the day resting and trying to recover. Jace asked Miriam to bring him clean cloths and cold water and he soothed their eyes for the rest of the day.

The next morning, Jace, Da, Ivan and William strolled through the city. After a couple of hours they arrived in the park. Finding a secluded spot under an oak tree, they sat down on the grass, William standing guard about twenty feet away.

"So, what do you think, guys?" Da said to the group.

Ivan looked at Da. "I might be able to remember the key. The password is most likely tied to my mother's birth date. I will try it. I don't think Richard fully understands what may happen, though. On some of the androids we tested H-11 on, they became aggressive. Some of them smashed things up and tried to harm people. We had to deactivate some and destroy others.

We shelved the project and felt it best to keep the top androids at H-10."

Da gazed at William who was staring in their direction. "What about William?"

"We can trust him, Da."

"Are you sure?"

"He has been my guard every day since I got here. He has even spoken privately against the King."

"Hmm. It could be a ruse, though. He could be gaining your trust. A good spy would do that. Are you one hundred and ten percent sure?"

"Yes, Da."

At that moment, William walked over and addressed the group. "Excuse me, but I couldn't help but overhear your conversation. I have enhanced hearing and the ability to read lips." He faced Da. "A good thing for you that Jace has told the truth. I *can* be trusted and am concerned about what the King is planning."

William now addressed the whole group: "During the war with the CRUD humans, Richard rose to prominence. Clones and loyal humans joined the androids in the short war. Richard was a fierce warrior, but after the great victory he eliminated his competitors and proclaimed himself King of Mars and formed a council. They started to build a new generation of androids, loyal to Richard and full of hate for most humans. Humans from other countries were allowed to live and work on Mars, but had to pay tribute to the new kingdom. Over the past few months, Richard relaxed restrictions and humans are now allowed to visit and live in Mars City.

"He also had a new android body built for himself— to be the tallest, *and* most handsome, in the land. But it isn't enough for him. He knows that he is somewhat limited in knowledge. He wants unlimited intelligence for who knows what. Perhaps to rule the entire Milky Way galaxy."

"It would be scary to give him the key," said Ivan.

"He will torture you if you do not," responded William.

Just then, Jace spotted Miriam strolling by on the main path, wearing an emerald dress. He pointed towards her. "Da, I want to talk to Miriam. She's also on our side."

"Okay, Sport. Be wise."

Jace ran off to catch up to her.

"Hey, Miriam."

She turned. "Jace. So good to see you here. I'm heading to the hill, would you like to join me?"

"Sure. I see you still have blue eyes today."

She gazed at him. "Yeah, I like the look. I think I'll keep them for a while. Do you like them?"

"Yeah." *Great. More guilt.*

A few minutes later, they sat at the top of the hill and Jace explained the meeting they just had below. He looked at her. "What do you think?"

She stared at the water. "The King does seem unstable these days, which is strange for an android.

He's getting worse, it seems. It's like he has a virus or something."

Jace nodded. "I'll mention that to Ivan."

"What is the plan for your little group?"

"I don't know yet. The men are discussing scenarios as we speak."

"Will you leave Mars as soon as the situation is resolved?"

"I suppose. But will the King let us leave?"

"Good question." She gazed at him through her dark bangs. "I have thought about some of the possibilities, while sitting endlessly in my room. If you do have to leave Mars suddenly, I want you to know that I will miss you."

"And I will miss you."

They both turned and looked at the fast-moving river.

After a few minutes, Jace said, "Let's go join the council. But I must swear you to secrecy."

She smiled. "You can trust me, Jace."

"I know." They headed back down the hill and joined the discussion.

"Da, Ivan, this is my friend, Miriam. She's the one who brought you water in the dungeon. She can be trusted."

"Hi, Miriam. Nice to meet you," responded Da.

"Hey, Miriam," said Ivan.

"Nice to meet you both," she replied. "Jace has told me a lot about you."

Jace turned towards Ivan. "Miriam thinks that the King might have a virus that is making him sick ... or crazy. However that works with androids."

"Yes, I have been thinkink the same," answered Ivan. "There's really somethink fundamentally wronk with him. Maybe they have been experimentink with their own keys and software, but it is not really workink. That would make sense."

"What should we do?" asked Da.

"I think we need to deactivate him," answered Ivan.

"That won't be easy," responded William. "He has spies and guards everywhere, and fiercely loyal subjects, not only with the androids, but also amongst the clones and humans."

Everyone stared at William and thought about his ominous words.

For the rest of that day and the next, the guests from Earth rested in their rooms and met in the park when they could, trying not to bring extra scrutiny upon themselves. When the two days were up, they were summoned to the King's conference room. As they entered, they viewed four royal androids, sporting magenta capes, sitting beside the King: two on either side. In behind them stood four royal guards with blue capes. William and Robin (the other guard from when Jace first arrived) stood at the side of the room and pointed the visitors towards their seats.

The King gestured with both arms. "This is my council. We want to know what you have decided,

Ivan Fedorov. Have you remembered the key?"

"I'm close. I remember that it has somethink to do with my mother's birth date, but it has been many years, and many bottles of whisky, since working on that project. I might not be able to retrieve it immediately."

BOOM! Richard smashed his fist on the table. "Guards, take Fedorov to the dungeon."

What?

"It won't help me to remember," responded Ivan.

The King glared at him. "You better hope it will. I hear that rats get into the dungeon from time to time. *Large rats*. The jailer tries to keep them out, but every once in a while one gets in. So, the sooner you can remember those passwords and codes the better it will be for you."

Rats? *Was he serious or bluffing*?

Richard pointed at Da. "Also, confine Mister Power to his room until we are finished with Fedorov."

William and Robin walked over to Da and Ivan. Da squeezed Jace's arm as if to say, don't worry, and stood as the guards marched him and Ivan out of the room.

The King looked at Jace. "You are free to go to your room."

Jace walked back to his room, dejected, and sat in the big comfy chair. Things were not going well. He thought for hours about what to do next. *Please God, help us*. Later, the buzzer sounded and he answered the portal. William entered, put a finger to his mouth and marched to the closet with Jace close behind. At the closet, William pulled out a gold sword hilt and handed it to him. *Whoa – a light sword!* It felt solid in his hand and had a black leather grip with a round emerald sensor. It was beyond cool.

"It's just in case. I had it custom made for you," William whispered. Jace hid the handle on a shelf behind some clothes and they walked back to the portal. William gazed at him. "Make sure you listen to him, for *Defender* is not your average smartsword." With that, William left.

Whoa! *The sword has a name*? Jace sat back in his chair and mused some more. The next morning, he went to breakfast as normal, but wasn't talkative. Only he and the King were present, and Jace didn't talk much out of spite. This was his way of being rebellious, without provoking the King's wrath and getting sent to the dungeon himself or locked in his room like Da.

After breakfast, he lay on his bed in his room. A few minutes later, the buzzer sounded. He answered and Miriam entered. "I brought you a cup of tea, sir." She pointed to a napkin and left.

As Jace drank his tea, he opened the napkin:

Hey, Sport. Hang in there. Love, Da

Jace was ecstatic. With the new sword and Da's note he suddenly felt confident. He walked to the spacious closet and stepped inside. *Well, Defender, what secrets do you possess*? Locating the hilt, he pressed the glowing emerald sensor. *Whoa*! Power rippled through the handle as a dazzling sapphire blade of light appeared, almost blinding him. *Awesome!* He turned it off immediately, placed it back on the shelf and stepped back into his room.

16

The King's Pride

The next morning, Jace's buzzer went off before breakfast and William stood before the portal. "There has been a development. The King requires everyone at breakfast immediately." Jace threw on his cloak and they departed right away. As he entered the dining hall, he was surprised to see Ivan and Da sitting at the table. *Wow.*

"I have great news," announced Richard, looking like the cat who swallowed the canary. "But first, everyone order your meals so the food will be on its way while we chat." He clapped and the servants entered and left again.

The King then made a sweeping arm gesture. "Fedorov, can you inform everyone of the fantastic news?"

All eyes turned to Ivan, who appeared dishevelled. "Sure. I remembered the key last night and informed the King. However, I wash my hands of all responsibility."

Richard smiled. "I will personally take that responsibility, Fedorov. I have informed my council and engineers, and later today we'll do a few experiments to see how the new coding performs."

"Are we free now?" asked Ivan.

"Yes. Let's just say you are under a form of house arrest until everything is verified. You have freedom in the castle and the city, but do not attempt to leave. You don't know it, but you have been monitored the entire time you've been here."

Jace gulped. *Was William or Miriam a double-agent? A traitor?*

An hour after breakfast they all met in the park again, in the same spot as before. William stood some distance away from the group so as not to show his hand and Miriam joined them a few minutes into the discussion.

Ivan frowned. "Sorry about that, guys. I couldn't take the dungeon anymore. Every sound I heard I thought of rats — big, hungry rats. Early this mornink, I informed the jailer and he told Richard. I was permitted to go to my room shortly after that. Sorry."

"You have nothing to be sorry about, my friend," said Da.

Everyone agreed and encouraged Ivan.

"Thanks. It will be interestink when they implement the higher intelligence this afternoon. At least I warned them. Keep your eyes open for any strange or unusual behaviour from Richard or whoever else they upload it on."

"If I see anything, I'll let Jace know immediately," responded Miriam.

Da nodded. "I hope the King will keep his word and let us go soon. We should make a backup plan just in case."

Everyone nodded.

The gang eventually returned to the castle and the humans visited each other in their rooms for the rest of the day, waiting to hear how the upgrade was going. They were kept in the dark until the following morning and were summoned to breakfast once again.

The beaming King was mum until everyone had ordered and were sipping their tea and coffee.

"My lord, when will we know how things are going and when we can leave?" asked Ivan.

"Oh, haven't you heard?" answered the King. "They finished uploading the new data last night. I am now the only android on Mars, and in the entire galaxy, who has been upgraded to H-11. In fact, it went so well, I taught the engineers how to upgrade the coding to H-12." He laughed.

Jace noticed that Richard's eyes and facial expressions were getting wilder. *Can an android be insane?*

"But that's crazy," blurted Ivan. "Level twelve has never been tried before."

The King smirked. "You humans are too cautious, Fedorov. I calculated the risks myself and ordered it done immediately. And as you can see, I'm perfectly fine. We'll keep you here for three more days in case we need you for anything further and then you are free to leave Mars."

Richard stood up with his hands on his hips and a huge grin on his face. "And as the benevolent King that I am, I give you the freedom of the kingdom until you leave."

He sat back down. "Alfred!"

The valet appeared. "Yes, my lord."

"I need you to plan a parade, immediately, in my honour, so that we may update my loyal subjects as to my new *galactic* intelligence."

"Yes, my lord."

With that, everyone was dismissed.

Announcements were made over the next two days about the parade, scheduled for Saturday. The castle and city became a beehive of activity with androids, clones and humans running here and there. New colourful banners were hung along Lionheart Boulevard and throughout the park. Jace's group planned to be there to take in the spectacle, which would end with a speech from the King at the large stage in the middle of the park.

The plan was for Jace, Da and Ivan to depart Mars on Sunday. It was going to be hard to say good-bye to Miriam and William, as they had become such close friends over this incredible time. The group took in more sights and visits to the park over the next two days, but change was in the air.

On Saturday morning, Jace popped into his dad's room, which was similar to his.

His father sat on the couch. "Are you ready to leave tomorrow?"

Throwing himself into the big chair, Jace answered: "Yeah. I can't wait to see Ma. I'll be a bit sad about leaving Miriam and William, though."

Da nodded. "I wanted to talk to you about Miriam."

Uh, oh.

"You two seem pretty close. Almost like—

"Don't say it, Da. I feel guilty enough already." He looked down.

"I see."

He gazed at his dad through his bangs. "How am I going to face Helena? What will I say?"

"Good questions."

"I need some dad advice."

His dad chuckled. "This is a tough one, Jace. I think we both need to think about it a bit more. I will try to give you some dad advice later in the day. For now, let's go enjoy breakfast and then the parade, and then get the heck out of here!"

"Sounds like a plan!"

They stood up and hugged. "Thanks, Da. It's so nice to know I can talk to you about this."

"Any time, Sport. That's what I'm here for."

Five minutes later, they sat at breakfast with Ivan. The King was absent, no doubt because of the preparations, so the team enjoyed a hearty breakfast, with Miriam serving them and William standing guard as usual.

Later, Jace stood in his room as he put on a new shirt. The buzzer sounded and he let in Miriam. She gestured to the closet. "Do you need new clothes, sir?"

Huh? Jace followed her.

She opened the door, stepped inside and turned to Jace, putting a finger to her mouth. "Richard had a strange power problem last evening at supper."

"Really? What happened?"

"I overheard two servants speaking about it this morning," she whispered. "He was sitting at the table, when suddenly the lights in his head started flickering more than usual. His eyes got very bright and then he lost power. His head banged on the table, just like he was knocked out or something."

"Whoa! I've got to tell Da and Ivan."

"Yes. He quickly came back to life and dismissed concerns, but had no real knowledge of what happened."

They gazed at each other. "Thank you, Miriam."

"Glad I could help." She smiled and left.

I'm going to miss her. A lot.

Jace's group had a great spot for the parade, about halfway down Lionheart. There were thousands and thousands of 'people' lining the streets: androids, clones and humans. Dignitaries came from all the colonies on Mars and a ton of androids and male clones had arrived into town from the mines. A few minutes later they could see the beginnings of the parade, as a squad of ARUs marched in front, followed by displays of fighter jets, missiles, drones and tanks.

After that came various decorated floats with androids, clones or humans waving to the spectators. The crowds cheered the various displays and marching bands. Finally, they spotted the King's entourage, with Richard sitting in an open horse-drawn red-and-gold carriage with mounted guards following. The King waved to his loyal subjects, who clapped and cheered wildly. Robin rode a decorated horse in front and shouted: "Bow the knee to his royal highness, Richard, Sovereign of Mars City and Planet." Everyone bowed as Richard approached, so Jace's group did as well.

As the carriage passed, the King suddenly slumped to his side. Spectators gasped and screamed. One of the royal guards tried to straighten him up, while William, Ivan and Da raced to the carriage. Jace and Miriam pushed through the crowd so they could view the event better.

"He's had a power outage," shouted Ivan. "Someone get his charger, immediately."

"We don't have one," replied Robin, who had arrived on the scene. "He was zapped in his room this morning."

At that moment, the King popped back to life, straightened up and stared at Ivan. "*What* are *you* doing?"

"He is trying to assist you, my lord," responded William.

"Arrest him, Robin! Fedorov is trying to kill me!"

"*What*?!" exclaimed Ivan.

"It's a coup!" the King shouted.

"It's a coup!" was repeated by many in the crowd, who glared at Ivan and Da.

"No, my King!" countered Robin. "I saw everything. You had a power problem. They came to assist you."

"Silence! Guards! Guards!" The royal guards surrounded the King with light-swords drawn. "Arrest them all!" He pointed at Ivan, Da and William. "This is a coup attempt. Arrest them for treason! Arrest Robin as well!"

The royal guards took them all away.

Jace was shocked and stared at Miriam. "What should we do?"

"Let's go back to the castle. I don't think anyone noticed us." He and Miriam drifted towards the back of the crowd, and then made it back to Mars Castle with no issues. Once inside, they went to Jace's room and spoke in hushed tones.

Miriam brushed dark locks out of her eyes. "Let me get back to my household chores, so no one suspects anything. You come to lunch as though everything is normal, and we'll just respond to the news as it comes in. Hopefully, the King will not arrest either of us."

"Good thinking. I guess Da and everyone will be in

the dungeon, again."

"Yes, I would think so."

He gazed at her. "Richard sure has a major power problem."

"Yes. His system seems way overloaded."

They both nodded.

She touched his arm "I should go, Jace. Be safe."

"You, too."

She left and Jace threw himself on the bed. *Thinking. Thinking. Thinking.*

A few minutes later, Jace opened his portal and listened. There was tons of activity in the hallways. He could hear footsteps and chatter far away, suddenly coming closer. He closed his portal. The sounds moved past his room. *Thank God.*

An hour later, his buzzer sounded and Miriam appeared. "The King requests your presence at lunch." She lowered her voice: "Everyone is in the dungeon. The parade was cancelled and all the subjects believe there was a coup attempt. They want the traitors publicly executed."

"They still do that?"

"Almost never, but yes. I have to go. See you at lunch."

A few minutes later, Jace sat with the King and many guards were stationed all over the room.

The King stared at him, but his eyes seemed off, almost weak. "Well, Jace. I suppose you have heard the news."

"Yes, my lord."

"I have taken a liking to you, young Jace. I hope that you won't follow in the footsteps of your traitorous father or Fedorov."

"No, my lord."

"All I require is loyalty, Jace. Will you be loyal to me?"

"Yes, of course, my lord. You know I love the kingdom."

"Good. Good. Alfred!"

"Yes, my lord."

"Get my zapper."

Alfred grabbed the lithium pack and gave Richard a good jolt.

"Ah, that feels great. You must have forgotten to zap me this morning."

Alfred glanced at Jace. "Yes, my lord. I am sorry. It will not happen again."

Oh my goodness. Jace stared at the King as a plan crystallized in his head.

17

Checkmate

Miriam walked down the dark narrow passageway carrying a jug of water.

The massive jailer outside the dungeon portal put up his hand and glared at her. "What's this?"

"Alfred told me to bring water to the prisoners."

"Why wasn't I informed?"

"Don't ask me." She put a hand on her hip and stared at him. "Well, what am I supposed to do with this water? Alfred *is* the King's trusted valet."

Staring at Miriam, he placed a finger under her chin. "My, you are a pretty lass."

She slapped his hand away, walked a few steps and turned back. "Keep your hands off me or you'll answer to the King."

He smirked. "Oh, will I? And who'll tell him?"

At that moment, Jace pressed the sensor on his sword to strike down the jailer from behind. However, the big man, alerted by the bright light, spun and blocked

Jace's attempt. *Boom*! The light swords clashing reverberated like thunder throughout the narrow hallway. After a few more attempts, Jace backed off.

The jailer grinned, raising his sword. "Going to run away, my little coward?"

Yeah, actually .... Jace ran about ten feet down the hallway, then turned back to face the jailer. *What am I going to do*? The man was much stronger, and good with a sword, and Jace had never used one before. Jace looked at Miriam, who was staring at him intently, as though trying to communicate something. At that moment, she poured water out of the ceramic mug. Sweating, and thinking of his dad who was right behind that portal, Jace gathered his courage and stepped towards the jailer.

The jailer threw his head back and laughed. "Come and get it, lad."

Jace, using speed and agility, tried every move he'd ever seen on a screen, but each strike and thrust was deflected. As the jailer now rained blows down on Jace, something incredible happened. *Defender* pulled Jace's hand this way and that — deflecting and blocking each strike. Jace, retreating with each blow, followed *Defender*'s lead as best he could, but knew he was in deep trouble. *Help me, God.* Backed into a corner, Jace crouched low, but kept *Defender* raised above his head for protection. In that moment, with his heart pounding, Jace looked up and noticed the emerald sensor flickering. *Why?*

Sensing victory, the jailer stopped for a moment to get in a last laugh. "You shouldn't send a boy to do a man's job!" With that, he raised his sword high above his head with two hands, as Jace gulped.

At that instant, Miriam smashed the large mug into the side of the jailer's head. The mug broke against his cheekbone and shattered on the stone floor. The bloodied man lowered his sword and turned towards Miriam, growling: "And you, my dear, will be next!"

As the jailer turned back towards Jace, Jace pointed the sword and pressed the emerald sensor. The blade of light ejected, plunging into the chest of the big man, who grunted in pain as his eyes bulged. The sapphire blade glowed brighter for a moment before disappearing. The jailer's sword clanged to the ground as he stumbled into the wall and crashed heavily on the stone floor — dead.

Jace stared at *Defender*'s hilt in disbelief.

Miriam raced around the body and flew into Jace's arms. They hugged tightly. "You did it, Jace. You did it!"

He smiled. "Actually *Defender* did it — *God* did it. I had no idea the sword was going to fire. The sensor was flashing. I had a feeling to point the sword and ...." In the glow of the torchlight, he gazed into her dark-blue eyes. He wanted to kiss her so bad, but stopped himself. He knew she felt the same.

"C'mon," Jace finally said, grabbing her hand, "We have to free the captives." He waved his hand over the portal sensor and jumped inside. "It's Jace," he said, as Miriam brought a torch into the room.

"Thank God!" shouted Da. Jace ran to his father and embraced him.

"Good show!" exclaimed William. "Get the master key from the jailer."

Jace went out, found the key and rushed back in, unlocking the captives one by one.

"Thanks," said Ivan, freed from arm chains once again.

Jace addressed William: "Alfred knows about the King's memory glitches."

"Good. Give me your sword," William replied.

"I fired the blade," responded Jace, thinking that *Defender* was now useless.

"There's always another one," replied William, who hit the sensor. Amazingly, a new blade appeared. He smiled at Jace and turned it off. "Go to the dining room and ask to speak to the King. We will enter the room and handle the situation."

"I'm so proud of you guys," said Da to Jace and Miriam.

"Hear, hear!" replied Robin.

Jace turned to Miriam who was beaming at him. A short time later, they climbed the stairs, while the rest of the gang followed behind.

Soon, Jace stood in the dining room. "Alfred!" he hollered.

The old valet appeared.

"I have something important to tell the King."

Alfred nodded and left.

A minute later, Richard appeared.

"What is it, young Jace?"

"Please sit down, my lord. I must tell you something important."

The King sat. "Yes? What is it?"

At that moment, William walked into the room. The King's eyes popped. From the other direction entered Robin.

The King rose. "What is this?"

"Don't bother calling the guards," said William. "It's over."

"*Whatever* are you talking about?"

Alfred entered the room. "My lord, you have a virus. A bad virus that is affecting your power and memory."

Richard smashed the table with his fist as the lights flickered on his forehead. "Lies! Lies!"

"No, my lord, it is true. You have a choice to make. You can go down in history as a cruel and evil tyrant or you can let us help you. What will it be? We have your best interests at heart."

The King sat down and sheepishly turned to Alfred. "Well, I have been feeling a bit off lately."

Alfred waved his arm. "Quickly, Ivan."

Ivan, Da and Miriam entered the room, with Ivan addressing Richard: "If you allow us to deactivate you, we can remove the hyper software and get rid of the virus. You will go back to how you used to be at level ten intelligence, but without the problems. I believe you will make a full recovery — so to speak."

"Will I lose my memory? I would not like that."

"No, you should be fine."

The King rested his head on the table, defeated. "So be it. Alfred, please call the engineers and give Fedorov full access."

"Yes, my lord." Alfred opened the panel on Richard's back and turned the King off.

18

Fare Thee Well

The sun sat low and distant on this cool blue-sky morning as Jace followed Da and Ivan through the line. The trio shook hands and said a few words to each person they passed.

Standing in front of Miriam, Jace gazed into her misty eyes as they held each other's arms. She looked like a bright flower in her magenta dress, her long black hair blowing in the light breeze. "Thank you for everything, Miriam. Take care."

"Return to me, Jace Power."

"I will try."

She managed a smile through her tears. "Fare thee well."

"Fare thee well."

Jace tore himself away and moved on to William. "It was great to meet you," Jace said to his favourite guard, tapping the hilt of his sword. "I will cherish this sword forever."

William smiled. "Good show. I am so glad to have met you, Jace. I think you have grown in the short time you have been here. You are turning into a fine young man — a courageous one at that."

"Thank you, William." They shook hands as he moved on to Robin.

"It was a pleasure to meet you, Jace. Fare thee well." They shook hands.

"Fare thee well," returned Jace.

Turning his attention to Alfred, he thanked him for everything.

Alfred inclined his head. "In spite of everything, I hope you enjoyed Mars City and the castle."

"I did, very much. I wouldn't change this adventure for anything."

Alfred smiled and nodded as Jace joined Ivan and Da in front of the King. Richard vigorously shook their hands. "I want to thank each one of you, again, for your assistance. Without your intervention, I don't know what would have been the fate of myself and the kingdom. It might sound strange, coming from an android, but I'm starting to believe in Providence. If I had not kidnapped Jace, you would not have arrived to save our kingdom."

"You're welcome, my lord," said each one. The King's transformation was astounding. Ivan had worked closely with the engineers for hours and had put Richard back together again. The viruses were eliminated and he now had a clean bill of health. With that, Jace and company walked up the stairs of the King's luxurious magenta ship and got ready for the long trip back to Earth. They would be dropped off on the moon and take the Comet home, which was attached to the back of the King's ship.

The three of them stopped at the top of the stairs and waved to their friends. It was like leaving family. Jace was glad he was going to have seven days to think about things on the way home. *Home.* It was surreal and hard to fathom. It really was two different worlds that he was living in. Da and Ivan entered the ship while Jace waved one last time to Miriam, remembering their special time together yesterday afternoon.

Jace and Miriam sat in their favourite spot atop Glasgow Hill, staring down at the lush scenery and river.

"Well, I guess this is our last day together," she said.

"I guess so." Jace was filled with sadness. He had grown accustomed to their time together, especially their wonderful chats. He would miss her greatly. He didn't know what to say or do. He felt trapped between Mars and Earth — between Miriam and Helena. What a conundrum. They sat there for fifteen minutes and didn't say another word.

Miriam finally broke the silence: "Will you ever return to Mars for a visit?"

"I sure hope so. It's only seven days away when you

think about it. Maybe you will visit Cape Breton one day."

"I would love to, although I don't know how I would ever accomplish that. I have no parents and very limited resources. I feel so alone. Now more than ever."

"I will try very hard to come back one day and visit. And every time I look at this cloak, I will think of you."

"Thank you, Jace. I will wait for your visit, just like a Jane Austen heroine."

They spent another hour on the bench and then strolled to the castle through the park and city. As they walked through town, Jace noticed the amusement park and thought that it might be great to go in. "Hey, want to go to the fair for an hour or two?"

"Sure."

The fair had giant anti-gravity Ferris balls with a great view of the city and lots of other rides and games to play. They jumped into a giant red ball for two and enjoyed the view from way up.

Later, Jace won a big polar bear stuffy at the laser blaster booth, shooting some wild looking alien graphics that attacked him from the ground and sky. Miriam giggled and cheered as he eliminated each one. It reminded him a lot of shooting the robots in Cape Breton.

After the female clone handed him the prize, he gazed at Miriam. "Would you like it?"

She smiled. "I'd love to have it."

He handed the bear to her and she hugged it and carried it for the rest of the afternoon. It was a fantastic day together, but it was also good-bye. Later that evening, Jace, Da, Ivan, and all their friends had a wonderful supper together and then the guests departed to their rooms to prepare to leave the next morning.

Jace snapped back to the present as Miriam wiped tears with a white handkerchief. At that moment, he heard Da calling: "We have to go, Jace."

As Jace started to turn, Miriam blew him a kiss. He touched his cheek as though he felt it. Walking into the spacecraft, he sat down in a large white seat beside Da as the portal sealed. A few minutes later, the android pilots started the engines, which roared to life. Jace gazed out his window, as Da put a big hand on his shoulder.

As they rolled down the tarmac, Jace, Da and Ivan waved out the windows as their friends waved back. The last person Jace saw on Mars was Miriam, waving her handkerchief, as the spaceship lifted off the surface and rocketed out the portal. *Fare thee well.*

Turn the page for a preview of Book 2.

JACE POWER

AND THE
MARS CITY COUP

JACE POWER

1
Dreams

December, 2139

Miriam, holding her white polar bear stuffy, with Jace sitting beside her, ascended in the shiny red Ferris ball higher and higher until they had a great view of the wondrous castle and city. Laughing, they pointed out various sites below. A short time later, they descended and Jace exited the big red ball, walking out the small metal gate. But, as he turned back, the android worker closed the gate and the red ball with Miriam still sitting in it rose again. What the?

"Return to me, Jace" she said over and over as she rose higher and higher.

"I will," replied Jace each time, watching her ascend. Adding to his exasperation was an incessant alarm ringing in his ears.

He awoke, his watch beeping loudly. He rolled over and tried to hit it twice, but finally grabbed it and shut it off. *Ugh!* The time read 9:20 and he was late for school!

"Jace," his mother hollered up the stairs, "get going, you're late!"

Ugh! He looked out the window. New snow covered the ground like a soft blanket. At least he could take his board.

"Wash up and get ready. I'll make you breakfast. No sense going to school on an empty stomach."

Jace forced himself to get ready, but all he wanted to do was sleep a little longer and dream a bit more about Miriam. Would he ever really see her again? The whole Mars adventure seemed like a distant dream. He finally bundled down the stairs, ate his brekkie and threw on his parka and backpack.

"What class do you have at ten?"

"Just homeroom."

"Oh, good, Miss Townsend will understand. You have an excellent attendance record otherwise."

Yeah. Jace was very happy he had his fave teacher again this year for homeroom.

"I put twenty dollars in your wallet to pay the school lunch program. Don't forget," his mother said as she gave him a peck on the cheek. Ma had been babying him since he had returned from Mars and had even refused to let him fly solo for six months afterwards.

He knew it was all in love, though. He smiled at her as he grabbed his board. "See you later, Ma."

Zipping up the road, Jace cut through Central School's grounds before making his way up Eighth

Street to BEC. The dream had jolted him back to Mars City and made him examine his feelings for Miriam once again. When they had finally made it home from Mars, his mother hugged him like she would never let him go. He had missed her so much. Ivan had gone over to Barb and Helena's and a few minutes later Helena had arrived at his house. They embraced, but he instantly knew that things had changed. He tried to hide his true feelings but could see in her eyes that she knew.

Both families and Ivan spent that first day together eating great food, with Jace, Da and Ivan recounting the saga – or most of it at least. And, as the days and months passed he kept his feelings for Miriam a secret. He didn't know if Da had told Ma, but suspected it. The great thing was that Da was just letting it all play out and was not giving him any 'Dad advice' without being asked. So he and Helena had resumed their normal 'good friends' relationship, but they were no longer boyfriend and girlfriend.

Jace's watch rang, so he stopped for a moment and took it.

His dad appeared. "Hey, Sport, heard you're just on your way to school." He chuckled.

Jace grinned. "Yeah, I slept in. What's up?"

"I have some very interesting news for you."

"What?"

"Someone tipped me off that President Franklin has invited King Richard to the US, where they're going to sign a historic agreement on trade and a military pact."

"Wow!"

"I know. Looks like we're going to see some of our Martian friends in the near future."

"Wow."

His dad nodded. "It's all top secret for now, until the media reports it, but I wanted you to know. Anyway, I have to get back to work."

"Love ya, Da."

"Love ya, Sport."

Jace continued up Eighth Street and closed in on BEC. He could see a few other students making their way to the entrance, so he was not the only one who had slept in on this frigid winter morning. As he hopped off his board and climbed the steps, he notice Mitch and his goons blocking the portal. Some of the students were trying to push by them, but the idiots were laughing and stopping them. As Jace approached, he smelled marijuana. *Great.* "Smoking pot at ten, boys?"

"What's it to ya, loser?" responded Mitch, standing in his way and snickering with his idiotic friends.

"I don't really care, Mitch. I just want to get to my class."

Mitch tried to get in his face, but he had stopped growing in the past year and Jace was now almost a full head taller.

"I heard you killed a man on Mars," Mitch said.

"Don't believe everything you hear."

Mitch glanced at his goons. "I didn't think so. I knew you didn't have it in you."

Jace really had no time for this nonsense this morning. He put his leg behind Mitch and pushed him backwards, tripping him. Jace hung onto him, though, as he didn't want Mitch to hit the concrete under the snow. The goons and other kids made all kinds of gasps and shrieks as Mitch fell.

As Jace stood back up, Mitch's buddies surrounded him. However, the portal slid open and there stood Miss Townsend with her hands on her hips. "What's going on here? And what's that awful stench? No one better be smoking on school property."

With that, the morons moved out of the way, and Jace and his schoolmates entered.

As Jace passed his fave teacher, she patted him on the back.

Other Books by Randall James

Youth & Family

The Hicks of Alpha Centauri

Gold & Sharpe

The Strikerz

Memoirs

Cape Breton Orphan
(Local Bestseller)

Cape Breton Orphan Returns

Randall James grew up on spectacular Cape Breton Island, NS, and now resides on beautiful Vancouver Island, BC.

www.ingramcontent.com/pod-product-compliance
Lightning Source LLC
Chambersburg PA
CBHW051923110726
47902CB00002B/399